GALACTIC POT-HEALER

'Dick was many authors: a poor man's Pynchon, an oracular postmodern, a rich product of the changing counter-culture' *Village Voice Literary Supplement*

'Dick is entertaining us about reality and madness, time and death, sin and salvation. [He is] our own homegrown Borges' Ursula K. Le Guin

'It's beginning to look as though greatness has been thrust upon Philip K. Dick . . . [He] has chosen to handle material too nutty to accept, too admonitory to forget, too haunting to abandon' *Washington Post*

'In all his work he was astonishingly intimate, self-exposed, and very dangerous. He was the funniest sf writer of his time, and perhaps the most terrifying. His dreads were our own, spoken as we could not have spoken them' *The Encyclopedia of Science Fiction*

'Dick quietly produced serious fiction in a popular form and there can be no greater praise'
Michael Moorcock

Also by Philip K. Dick

NOVELS

Solar Lottery (1955)
The World Jones Made (1956)
The Man Who Japed (1956)
The Cosmic Puppets (1957)
Eye in the Sky (1957)
Dr Futurity (1959)
Time Out of Joint (1959)
Vulcan's Hammer (1960)
The Man in the High Castle (1962)
The Game-Players of Titan (1963)
The Penultimate Truth (1964)
The Simulacra (1964)
Martian Time-Slip (1964)
Clans of the Alphane Moon (1964)
Dr Bloodmoney, or How We Got Along After the Bomb (1965)
The Three Stigmata of Palmer Eldritch (1965)
Now Wait for Last Year (1966)
The Crack in Space (1966)
The Ganymede Takeover (with Ray F. Nelson) (1967)
The Zap Gun (1967)
Counter-Clock World (1967)
Do Androids Dream of Electric Sheep? (1968)
Ubik (1969)
Our Friends From Frolix 8 (1970)
A Maze of Death (1970)
We Can Build You (1972)
Flow My Tears, The Policeman Said (1974)
Confessions of a Crap Artist (1975)

Deus Irae (with Roger Zelazny) (1976)
A Scanner Darkly (1977)
The Divine Invasion (1981)
Valis (1981)
The Transmigration of Timothy Archer (1982)
Lies, Inc (1984)
The Man Whose Teeth Were All Exactly Alike (1984)
Puttering About in a Small Land (1985)
In Milton Lumky Territory (1985)
Radio Free Albemuth (1985)
Humpty Dumpty in Oakland (1986)
Mary and the Giant (1987)
The Broken Bubble (1988)

SHORT STORY COLLECTIONS

The Variable Man (1957)
A Handful of Darkness (1966)
The Turning Wheel (1977)
The Best of Philip K. Dick (1977)
The Golden Man (1980)
Minority Report (2002)

THE COLLECTED STORIES OF PHILIP K. DICK

1. Beyond Lies the Wub (1987)
2. Second Variety (1987)
3. The Father Thing (1987)
4. The Days of Perky Pat (1987)
5. We Can Remember it for You Wholesale (1987)

GALACTIC POT-HEALER

Philip K. Dick

The right of Philip K. Dick to be identified as the
author of this work has been asserted by him in accordance
with the Copyright, Designs and Patents Act 1988.

This edition published in Great Britain in 2005 by
Gollancz
An imprint of the Orion Publishing Group
Orion House, 5 Upper St Martin's Lane, London WC2H 9EA

1 3 5 7 9 10 8 6 4 2

A CIP catalogue record for this book is
available from the British Library

ISBN 0 575 07462 0

Printed in Great Britain by
Clays Ltd, St Ives plc

www.orionbooks.co.uk

For Cynthia Goldstone

And truly I was afraid, I was most afraid,
But even so, honoured still more
That he should seek my hospitality
From out the dark door of the secret earth

D. H. LAWRENCE

1

His father had been a pot-healer before him. And so he, too, healed pots, in fact any kind of ceramic ware left over from the Old Days, before the war, when objects had not always been made out of plastic. A ceramic pot was a wonderful thing, and each that he healed became an object which he loved, which he never forgot; the shape of it, the texture of it and its glaze, remained with him on and on.

However, almost no one needed his work, his services. Too few ceramic pieces remained, and those persons who owned them took great care to see that they did not break.

I am Joe Fernwright, he said to himself. I am the best pot-healer on Earth. I, Joe Fernwright, am not like other men.

Around in his office, cartons—empty—lay piled. Steel cartons, within which to return the healed pot. But on the incoming side—almost nothing. For seven months his bench had been bare.

During those months he had thought many things. He had thought that he ought to give up and take some other line of work onto himself—any line of work, so that he could go off the war veterans' dole. He had thought, *My work isn't good enough; I have virtually no clients because they are sending their broken pots to other firms to fix.* He had thought of suicide. Once, he had thought of a major crime, of killing someone high up in the hierarchy of the Peaceful International World Senate. But what good would that do? And anyhow life wasn't absolutely worth nothing, because there was one good thing which remained, even though everything else had evaded or ignored him. The Game.

On the roof of his rooming house, Joe Fernwright waited, lunch pail in hand, for the rapid-transit hover blimp to arrive. The cold morning air nipped and touched him; he shivered. It'll show up any time now, Joe informed himself. Except that it'll be full. And so it won't stop; it'll blipple on by, crammed to the brim. Well, he thought, I can always walk.

He had become accustomed to walking. As in every other field the government had failed miserably in the matter of public transportation. Damn them, Joe said to himself. Or rather, he thought, damn us. After all, he, too, was a part of the planetwide Party apparatus, the network of tendrils which had penetrated and then in loving convulsion clasped them in a hug of death as great as the entire world.

"I give up," the man next to him said with an irritable twitch of shaved and perfumed jowls. "I'm going to slide down the slide to ground level and walk. Lots of luck." The man pushed his way through the throng of those waiting for the hover blimp; the throng flowed together once more, behind him, and he was gone from sight.

Me, too, Joe decided. He headed for the slide, and so did several other grumpy commuters.

At street level he straddled a cracked and unrepaired sidewalk, took a deep angry breath, and then, via his personal legs, started north.

A police cruiser soared down to linger a little above Joe's head. "You're walking too slow," the uniformed officer informed him, and pointed a Walters & Jones laser pistol at him. "Pick up speed or I'll book you."

"I swear to god," Joe said, "that I'll hurry. Just give me time to pick up my pace; I just now started." He speeded up, phased himself with the other swiftly striding peds— those others lucky enough, like himself, to have jobs, to have somewhere to go on this dingy Thursday morning in early April 2046, in the city of Cleveland in the Communal North American Citizens' Republic. Or, he thought, at least to have something that *looks* like a job anyhow. A place, a talent, experience, and, one day soon, an order to fill.

His office and workroom—a cubicle, really—contained a bench, tools, the piles of empty metal boxes, a small desk, and his ancient chair, a leather-covered rocking chair which had belonged to his grandfather and then, at last, his father. And now he himself sat on that chair—sat day in, day out, month in, month out. He had, also, a single ceramic vase, short and portly, finished in a free-dripping dull blue glaze over the white biscuit; he had found it years ago and recognized it as seventeenth-century Japanese. He loved it. And it had never been broken, not even during the war.

He seated himself now in this chair and felt it give here and there as it adjusted itself to a familiar body. The chair knew him as well as he knew the chair; it had known him all his life. Then he reached to press the button which would bring the morning's mail sliding down the tube to his desk— reached, but then waited. What if there's nothing? he asked himself. There never is. But this could be different; it's like a batter: when he hasn't hit for a long time you say, "He's due any time now," and so he is. Joe pressed the button.

Three bills slid out.

And, with them, the dingy gray packet containing today's government money, his daily dole. Government paper money, in the form of odd and ornate and nearly worthless inflationary trading stamps. Each day, when he received his gray packet of newly printed notes, he hiked as rapidly as possible to GUB, the nearest all-purpose supershopping-redemptioncenter, and transacted hasty business: he swapped the notes, while they still had any worth, for food, magazines, pills, a new shirt—*anything*, in fact, tangible. Everyone did it. Everyone had to; holding onto government notes for even twenty-four hours was a self-imposed disaster, a kind of mortal suicide. Roughly, in two days government money dropped eighty percent in its redemptive power.

The man in the cubicle next to his called, "To the President's healthful longevity." A routine greeting.

"Yeah," Joe answered reflexively. Other cubicles, lots of them, level upon level. Suddenly a thought came to him. Exactly how many cubicles were there in the building? A thousand? Two or two-point-five thousand? I can do that today, he said to himself; I can investigate and find out how many other cubicles there are in addition to mine. Then I'll know how many people are with me here in this building . . . excluding those who are off sick or have died.

But first, a cigarette. He got out a package of tobacco cigarettes—highly illegal, due to the health hazard and the addictive nature of the plant in question—and started to light up.

At that moment his gaze fell, as always, on the smoke sensor mounted on the wall across from him. One puff, ten poscreds, he said to himself. Therefore he returned, then, the cigarettes to his pocket, rubbed his forehead ruthlessly, trying to fathom the craving lodged deep within him, the need which had caused him to break that law several times. What do I really yearn for? he asked himself. That for which oral gratification is a surrogate. Something vast, he decided; he felt the primordial hunger gape, huge-jawed, as if to cannibalize everything around him. To place what was outside inside.

Thus he played; this had created, for him, The Game.

Pressing the red button he lifted the receiver and waited

while the creaking, slow relay machinery fed his phone an outside line.

"Squeeg," the phone said. Its screen displayed nonobjective colors and segments. Electronic crosstalk made blurrily visible.

From memory he dialed. Twelve numbers, starting with the three which connected him with Moscow.

"Vice-Commissioner Saxton Gordon's staff calling," he said to the Russian switchboard officer whose face glowered at him from the miniature screen. "More games, I suppose," the operator said.

Joe said, "A humanoid biped cannot maintain metabolic processes by means of plankton flour merely."

After a glare of puritanical disapproval, the officer connected him with Gauk. The lean, bored face of the minor Soviet official confronted him. Boredom at once gave way to interest. "A preslávni vityaz," Gauk intoned. "Dostoini konovód tolpi byezmózgloi, prestóopnaya—"

"Don't make a speech," Joe interrupted, feeling impatient. As well as surly. This was his customary morning mood.

"Prostitye," Gauk apologized.

"Do you have a title for me?" Joe asked; he held his pen ready.

"The Tokyo translating computer has been tied up all morning," Gauk answered. "So I put it through the smaller one at Kobe. In some respects Kobe is more—how shall I put it?—quaint than Tokyo." He paused, consulting a slip of paper; his office, like Joe's, consisted of a cubicle, containing only a desk, a phone, a straight-backed chair made of plastic and a note pad. "Ready?"

"Ready." Joe made a random scratch-mark with his pen.

Gauk cleared his throat and read from his slip of paper, a taut grin on his face; it was a sleek expression, as if he were certain of himself on this one. "This originated in your language," Gauk explained, honoring one of the rules which all of them together had made up, the bunch of them scattered here and there across the map of Earth, in little offices, in puny positions, with nothing to do, no tasks or sorrows or difficult problems. Nothing but the harsh vacuity of their collective society, which each in his own way objected to, which all of them, in collaboration, circumvented by means of The Game. "Book title," Gauk continued. "That's the only clue I'll give you."

"Is it well known?" Joe asked.

Ignoring his question, Gauk read from the slip of paper. " 'The Lattice-work Gun-stinging Insect.' "

"Gun-slinging?" Joe asked.

"No. Gun-stinging."

" 'Lattice-work,' " Joe said, pondering. "Network. 'Stinging Insect.' Wasp?" He scratched with his pen, stumped. "And you got this from the translation computer at Kobe? Bee," he decided. " 'Gun,' so Gun-bee. Heater-bee. Laser-bee. Rod-bee. *Gat.*" He swiftly wrote that down. "Gat-wasp, gat-bee. Gatsby. 'Lattice-work.' That would be a grating. Grate." He had it now. "*The Great Gatsby,* by F. Scott Fitzgerald." He tossed down his pen in triumph.

"Ten points for you," Gauk said. He made a tally. "That puts you even with Hirshmeyer in Berlin and slightly ahead of Smith in New York. You want to try another?"

Joe said, "I have one." From his pocket he got out a folded sheet; spreading it out on his desk he read from it, " 'The Male Offspring in Addition Gets Out of Bed.' " He eyed Gauk then, feeling the warmth of knowledge that he had gotten a good one—this, from the larger language-translating computer in downtown Tokyo.

"A phononym," Gauk said effortlessly. "Son, sun. *The Sun Also Rises.* Ten points for me." He made a note of that.

Angrily, Joe said, "Those for Which the Male Homosexual Exacts Transit Tax."

"Another by Serious Constricting-path," Gauk said, with a wide smile. *"For Whom the Bell Tolls."*

" 'Serious Constricting-path'?" Joe echoed wonderingly.

"Ernest Hemingway."

"I give up," Joe said. He felt weary; Gauk, as usual, was far ahead of him in their mutual game of retranslating computer translations back into the original tongue.

"Want to try another?" Gauk asked silkily, his face bland.

"One more," Joe decided.

"Quickly Shattered at the Quarreling Posterior."

"Jesus," Joe said, with deep and timid bewilderment. It rang no bell, no bell at all. " 'Quickly shattered.' Broken, maybe. Broke, break. *Quick*—that would be fast. Breakfast. But 'Quarreling Posterior'?" He cogitated quickly, in the Roman sense. "Fighting. Arguing. Spat." In his mind no solution appeared. " 'Posterior.' Rear end. Ass. Butt." For a time he meditated in silence, in the Yoga fashion. "No," he said finally. "I can't make it out. I give up."

"So soon?" Gauk inquired, raising an eyebrow.

"Well, there's no use sitting here the rest of the day working that one over."

"Fanny," Gauk said.

Joe groaned.

"You groan?" Gauk said. "At one you missed that you should have got? Are you tired, Fernwright? Does it wear you out to sit there in your cubbyhole, doing nothing hour after hour, like the rest of us? You'd rather sit alone in silence and not talk to us? Not try anymore?" Gauk sounded seriously upset; his face had become dark.

"It's just that it was an easy one," Joe said lamely. But he could see that his colleague in Moscow was not convinced. "Okay," he continued. "I'm depressed. I can't stand this much longer. Do you know what I mean? You do know." He waited. A faceless moment poured past in which neither of them spoke. "I'm ringing off," Joe said, and began to hang up.

"Wait," Gauk said rapidly. "One more."

Joe said, "No." He hung up, sat emptily staring. On his unfolded sheet of paper he had several more, but— It's gone, he said to himself, bitterly. The energy, the capacity to fiddle away a lifetime without dignified work, and, in its place, the performance of the trivial, even the voluntarily trivial, as we have constructed here in The Game. Contact with others, he thought; through The Game our isolation is lanced and its body broken. We peep out, but what do we see, really? Mirror reflections of our own selves, our bloodless, feeble countenances, devoted to nothing in particular, insofar as I can fathom it. Death is very close, he thought. When you think in this manner. I can feel it, he decided. How near I am. Nothing is killing me; I have no enemy, no antagonist; I am merely expiring, like a magazine subscription: month by month. Because, he thought, I am too hollowed out to participate any longer. Even if they—the others who play The Game—need me, need my corny contribution.

And yet, as he gazed sightlessly down at his piece of paper, he felt dim action occurring within him, a kind of photosynthesis. A gathering of remaining powers, on an instinctive basis. Left alone, functioning in its sightless way, the biological effort of his body asserted itself physically; he began to jot a further title.

Dialing his phone, he obtained a satellite relay to Japan; he raised Tokyo and gave the digits for the Tokyo translating computer. With the skill of long habit he obtained a direct line to the great, clanking, booming construct; he bypassed its host of attendants.

"Oral transmission," he informed it.

The hulking GX9 computer clicked over to oral, rather than visual, reception.

"The Corn Is Green," Joe said. He turned on the recording unit of his phone.

At once the computer answered, giving the Japanese equivalent.

"Thank you and out," Joe said, and rang off. He then dialed the translating computer at Washington, D.C. Rewinding the tape of his phone recorder he fed the Japanese words—again in oral form—to the computer segment which would translate the Japanese utterance into English.

The computer said, "The cliché is inexperienced."

"Pardon?" Joe said, and laughed. "Repeat, please."

"The cliché is inexperienced," the computer said with god-like nobility and patience.

"That's an exact translation?" Joe inquired.

"The cliché is—"

"Okay," Joe said. "Sign off." He hung up and sat grinning; his energy, aroused by human amusement, surged up and invigorated him.

For a moment he sat hesitating, deciding, and then he dialed good ol' Smith in New York.

"Office of Procurement and Supply, Wing Seven," Smith said; his beaglelike face, haunted by ennui, manifested itself on the little gray screen. "Oh, hey there, Fernwright. Got something for me?"

"An easy one," Joe said. " 'The Cliché Is—' "

"Wait'll you hear mine," Smith interrupted. "Me first; come on, Joe—this is a great one. You'll never get it. Listen." He read swiftly, stammering over the words. "Bogish Persistentisms. By Shaft Tackapple."

"No," Joe said.

"No what?" Smith glanced up, frowning. "You haven't tried; you just sit there. I'll give you time. The rules say five minutes; you've got five minutes."

Joe said, "I'm quitting."

"Quitting what? The Game? But you're way up there!"

"I'm quitting my profession," Joe said. "I'm going to give up this work area and I'm going to cancel on my phone. I won't be here; I won't be able to play." He took a plunging breath, then spoke on. "I've saved up sixty-five quarters. Prewar. It took me two years."

"*Coins?*" Smith gaped at him. "*Metal* money?"

"It's in an asbestos sack under the radiator in my housing room," Joe said. I'll consult it today, he said to himself.

"There's a booth down the street from my room, at the intersection," he said to Smith. I wonder, he thought, if in the final analysis I have enough coins. They say Mr. Job gives so little; or, put another way, costs so much. But sixty-five quarters, he thought; that's plenty. That's equal to—he had to calculate it on his note pad. "Ten million dollars in trading stamps," he told Smith. "As per the exchange rate of today, as posted in the morning newspaper . . . which is official."

After a grinding pause, Smith said slowly, "I see. Well, I wish you luck. You'll get twenty words from it, for what you've saved up. Maybe two sentences. 'Go to Boston. Ask for—' and then it clicks off; then it'll cap the lid. The coinbox will rattle; your quarters will be down there in that maze of viaducts, rolling under hydraulic pressure to the central Mr. Job in Oslo." He rubbed beneath his nose, as if wiping away moisture, like a schoolboy heavy with rote-labor. "I envy you, Fernwright. Maybe two sentences from it will be enough. I consulted it, once. I handed fifty quarters over to it. 'Go to Boston,' it said. 'Ask for—' and then it shut off, and I felt as if it enjoyed it. That it liked to shut off, as if my quarters had stirred it to pleasure, the kind of pleasure a pseudolife-form would relish. But go ahead."

"Okay," Joe said stoically.

"When it's used up your quarters—" Smith continued, but Joe broke in, his voice blistered with harshness.

"I get your point," Joe said.

Smith said, "No prayers—"

"Okay," Joe said.

There was a pause as the two of them faced each other.

"No prayers," Smith said at last, "no nothing, will get that godbedamned machine to spit out one additional word."

"Hmm," Joe said. He tried to sound casual, but Smith's words had had their effect; he felt himself cool off. He experienced the winds, the howling gales, of fright. Anticipation, he thought, of winding up with nothing. A truncated partial statement from Mr. Job, and then, as Smith says—

blam. Mr. Job, turning itself off, is the ultimate visage of black iron, old iron from antediluvian times. The ultimate rebuff. If there is a supernatural deafness, he thought, it is that: when the coins you are putting into Mr. Job run out.

Smith said, "Can I—hurriedly—give you one more I've got? This came via the Namangan translator. Listen." He pawed feverishly with long, classic fingers at his own folded sheet of paper. " 'The Chesspiece Made Insolvent.' Famous movie circa—"

"The Pawnbroker," Joe said tonelessly.

"Yes! You're right there on it, Fernwright, really right there and swinging both arms and a tail as well. Another? Don't hang up! I have a truly good one, here!"

"Give it to Hirshmeyer in Berlin," Joe said, and hung up.

I am dying, he said to himself.

Seated there, in the tattered, antiquated chair, he saw, dully, that the red warning light of his mail tube had come on, presumably as of the last few minutes. Odd, he thought. There's no delivery until one-fifteen this afternoon. He thought, *Special delivery?* And punched the button.

A letter rolled out. Special delivery.

He opened it. Inside, a slip of paper. It said:

POT-HEALER, I NEED YOU. AND I WILL PAY.

No signature. No address except his, as destination. My god, he thought, this is something real and big. I know it.

He carefully moved his chair around so that he faced the red warning light of the mail tube. And prepared to wait. Until it comes, he said to himself. Unless I physically starve to death first. I will not voluntarily die, now, he thought harshly. I want to stay alive. And wait. And wait.

He waited.

2

Nothing more came down the mail tube that day and Joe Fernwright trudged "home."

"Home" consisted of a room on a subsurface level of a huge apartment building. Once, the Jiffi-view Company of Greater Cleveland came by every six months and created a 3-D projection, animated, of a view of Carmel, California. This "view" filled his room's "window," or ersatz window. However, of late, due to his bad financial situation, Joe had given up trying to imagine that he lived on a great hill with a view of the sea and of towering redwoods; he had become content—or rather resigned—to face blank, inert, black glass. And in addition, if that wasn't enough, he had let his psycho-lease lapse: the encephalic gadget installed in a closet of his room which, while he was "home," compelled his brain to believe that his ersatz view of Carmel was authentic.

The delusion was gone from his brain and the illusion was gone from his window. Now, "home" from work, he sat in a state of depression, reflecting, as always, on the futile aspects of his life.

Once, the Cleveland Historical Artifacts Museum had sent him regular work. His hot-needle device had melded many fragments, had re-created into a single homogeneous unit one ceramic item after another as his father had before him. But that was over, now; all the ceramic objects owned by the museum had been healed.

Here, in his lonely room, Joe Fernwright contemplated the lack of ornamentation. Time after time, wealthy owners of precious and broken pots had come to him, and he had done what they wanted; he had healed their pots, and they had gone away. Nothing remained after them; no pots to grace his room in place of the window. Once, seated like this, he had pondered the heat-needle which he made use of. If I press this little device against my breast, he had ruminated, and turn it on, and put it near my heart, it would put an end to me in less than a second. It is, in some ways, a powerful tool. The failure which is my life, he had thought again and again, would cease. Why not?

But there was the strange note which he had received in the mail. How had the person—or persons—heard of him? To get clients he ran a perpetual small ad in *Ceramics Monthly* . . . and via this ad the thin trickle of work, throughout the years, had come. Had come and now, really, had gone. But *this*. The strange note!

He picked up the receiver of his phone, dialed, and in a few seconds faced his ex-wife, Kate. Blond and hard lined, she glared at him.

"Hi," he said, in a friendly sort of fashion.

"Where's last month's alimony check?" Kate said.

Joe said, "I'm onto something. I'll be able to pay all my back alimony if this—"

"This what?" Kate interrupted. "Some new nuthead idea dredged out of the depths of what you call your brain?"

"A note," he said. "I want to read it to you to see if you can infer anything more from it than I can." His ex-wife, although he hated her for it—and for a lot more—had a quick mind. Even now, a year after their divorce, he still relied on her powerful intellect. It was odd, he had once thought, that you could hate a person and never want to see them again, and yet at the same time seek them out and ask their advice. Irrational. Or, he thought, is it a sort of super-rationality? To rise above hate . . .

Wasn't it the hate which was irrational? After all, Kate had never done anything to him—nothing except make him excessively aware, intently aware, always aware, of his inability to bring in money. She had taught him to loathe himself, and then, having done that, she had left him.

And he still called up and asked for her advice.

He read her the note.

"Obviously it's illegal," Kate said. "But you know your business affairs don't interest me. You'll have to work it out by yourself or with whoever you're currently sleeping with, probably some eighteen-year-old girl who doesn't know any better, who doesn't have any basis for comparison as an older woman would have."

"What do you mean 'illegal'?" he asked. "What kind of pot is illegal?"

"Pornographic pots. The kind the Chinese made during the war."

"Oh Christ," he said; he hadn't thought of that. Who but Kate would remember those! She had been lewdly fascinated by the one or two of them which had passed through his hands.

"Call the police," Kate said.

"I—"

"Anything else on your mind?" Kate said. "Now that you've interrupted my dinner and the dinner of everyone who's over here tonight?"

"Could I come over?" he said; loneliness crept through him and edged his question with the fear which Kate had always detected: the fear that she would retract into her implacable chesspiece fort, the fort of her own mind and body out of which she ventured to inflict a wound, or two, and then disappear back in, leaving an expressionless mask to greet him. And, by means of that mask, she used his own failings to injure him.

"No," Kate said.

"Why not?"

"Because you have nothing to offer anyone in the way of talk or discussion or ideas. As you've said many times, your talent is in your hands. Or did you intend to come over and break one of my cups, my Royal Albert cups with the blue glaze, and then heal it? As a sort of magical incantation designed to throw everyone into fits of laughter."

Joe said, "I can contribute verbally."

"Give me an example."

"What?" he said, staring at her face on the screen of the phone.

"Say something profound."

"You mean right now?"

Kate nodded.

"Beethoven's music is firmly rooted in reality. That's what makes him unique. On the other hand, genius as he was, Mozart—"

"Shove it," Kate said and hung up; the screen went blank.

I shouldn't have asked if I could come over, Joe realized with acute misery. It gave her that opening, that foot-in-the-psychic-door that she uses, that she preys on. Christ, he thought. Why did I ask? He got up and wandered drearily about his room; his motion became more and more aimless until at last he stopped and simply stood. I have to think about what really matters, he told himself. Not that she hung up or said anything nasty, but whether or not that note I got in the mail today means anything. Pornographic pots, he said to himself. She's probably right. And it's illegal to heal a pornographic pot, so there goes that.

I should have realized it as soon as I read the note, he said to himself. But that's the difference between Kate and me. She would know right away. I probably wouldn't have known until I had finished healing it and then taken a good firm look at it. I'm just not bright, he said to himself. Compared to her. Compared to the world.

"The arithmetical total ejaculated in a leaky flow," he thought fiercely. My best. At least I'm good at The Game. So what? he asked himself. *So what?*

Mr. Job, he thought, help me. The time has come. Tonight.

Going rapidly into the tiny bathroom attached to his room he grabbed up the lid of the water closet of the toilet. Nobody, he had often thought, looks into a toilet. There hung the asbestos sack of quarters.

And, in addition, a small plastic container floated. He had never seen it before in his life.

Lifting it from the water he saw, with disbelief, that it contained a rolled up piece of paper. A note, floating in the water closet of his toilet, like a bottle launched at sea. Oh, this can't really be, he thought, and felt like laughing. I mean Christ; it just can't. But he did not laugh, because he felt fear. Fear that bordered on dread. It's another communication, he said to himself. Like the one in the mail tube today. But nobody communicates this way; it isn't human!

He unscrewed the lid of the small plastic container and groped the enclosed piece of paper out. Yes, it had writing on it; he was right. He read the writing and then he read it again.

I WILL PAY YOU THIRTY-FIVE THOUSAND CRUMBLES

What in god's name is a crumble? he asked himself, and the dread sharpened into panic; he felt undernourished, strangulated heat rise to the back of his neck, a weak response somatically: his body, as well as his mind, was trying to adjust to this; it could not be done on a mental level alone, not this.

Returning to the main room he picked up the receiver of the phone and dialed the twenty-four-hour-a-day dictionary service.

"What's a crumble?" he asked, when the robot monitor answered.

"A crumbling substance," the computer fed to the monitor. "In other words fine debris. A small crumb or particle. Introduced into English 1577."

"Other languages?" Joe asked.

"Middle English kremelen. Old English gecrymian. Middle High Gothic—"

"What about non-Terran languages?"

"On Betelgeuse seven in the Urdian tongue it means a small opening of a temporary nature: a wedge which—"

"That's not it," Joe said.

"On Rigel two it means a small life-form which scuttles—"

"Not that either," Joe said.

"On Sirius five, in the Plabkian tongue 'crumble' is a monetary unit."

"That's it," Joe said. "Now tell me how much in Earth money thirty-five thousand crumbles represents."

The dictionary robot said, "I am sorry, sir, but you will have to consult the banking service for that answer. Please look in your phone book for the number." It clicked off; the screen died away.

He looked up the number and dialed the banking service.

"We are closed for the night," the banking-service robot monitor informed him.

"All over the world?" Joe said in amazement.

"Everywhere."

"How long do I have to wait?"

"Four hours."

"My life, my entire future—" But he was talking into a dead phone. The banking-service system had abolished the contact.

• • •

What I'll do, he decided, is lie down and sleep for four hours. It was now seven o'clock; he could set the alarm for eleven.

A pressing of the proper button brought the bed sliding out from the wall, virtually to fill the room; it had been his living room and now it was his bedroom. Four hours, he said to himself as he set the mechanism of the bed's clock. He lay down, made himself comfortable—as much so as the inadequate bed permitted—and groped for the toggle switch that induced immediately and powerfully the most profound sleep state possible.

A buzzer sounded.

The damn dream circuit, he said to himself. Even early like this do I have to use it? He leaped up, opened the cabinet beside the bed and got out the instructions. Yes, mandatory dreaming was required at any time he used the bed . . . unless, of course, he threw the sex lever. I'll do that, he said to himself. I'll tell it I'm having knowledge in the Biblical sense of a female person.

Once more he lay down and activated the sleep switch.

"You weigh one hundred and forty pounds," the bed said. "And there is exactly that weight extended over me. Therefore you are not engaged in copulation." The mechanism voided his throwing of the sleep toggle switch, and at the same time the bed began to warm up; the heating coils in it blatantly glowed beneath him.

He could not argue with an angry bed. So he turned on the sleep-dream interaction and shut his eyes, resignedly.

Sleep came at once; it always did: the mechanism was perfect. And, at once, the dream—which everyone anywhere in the world who was now asleep was also dreaming—clicked on.

One dream for everyone. But, thank god, a different dream each night.

"Hello, there," a cheerful dream-voice declared. "To-night's dream was written by Reg Baker and is called *In*

Memory Engraved. Now remember, folks; send in your dream ideas and win huge cash prizes! And if your dream is used you receive an all-expense paid trip off Earth entirely— in any direction you desire!"

The dream began.

Joe Fernwright stood before the Supreme Fiduciary Council in a state of trembling awe. The Secretary of the S.F.C. read from a prepared statement. "Mr. Fernwright," he declared in a solemn voice, "you have, in your engraving shop, created the plates from which the new money will be printed. Your design, out of over one hundred thousand presented to us, and many of them created with what must be called fantastic cunning, has won. Congratulations, Mr. Fernwright." The Secretary beamed at him in a fatherly manner, reminding him a little of the Padre presence, which he now and then made use of.

"I am pleased and honored," Joe responded, "by this award, and I know that I have done my part to restore fiscal stability to the world as we know it. It little matters to me that my face will be pictured on the brightly colored new money, but since it is so, let me express my pleasure at this honor."

"Your signature, Mr. Fernwright," the Secretary reminded him, in the fashion of a wise father. "Your signature, not your face, will appear on the currency notes. Where did you get the idea that it would be your likeness as well?"

"Perhaps you don't understand me," Joe said. "Unless my face appears on the new currency I will withdraw my design, and the entire economic structure of the Earth will collapse, seeing as how you'll have to go on using the old inflationary money which has by now become virtually waste paper to be thrown away at the first opportunity."

The Secretary pondered. "You would withdraw your design?"

"You read me loud and clear," Joe, in his dream, in *their*

dream, said. At this same moment roughly one billion other people on Earth were withdrawing their designs as he now was doing. But of course he had no thought of that; he only knew this: without him the system, the whole nature of their corporate state, would break apart. "And as to my signature, I will, as that great dead hero of the past Ché Guevara did, that noble person, that fine man who died for his friends, because of memory of him I will merely write 'Joe' on the bills. But my face must be of several colors. Three at least."

"Mr. Fernwright," the Secretary said, "you strike a hard bargain. You are a firm man. You do, in fact, remind me of Ché, and I think all the millions watching on TV will agree. Let's hear it now for Joe Fernwright and Ché Guevara both together!" The Secretary threw aside his prepared statement and began to clap. "Let's hear it out there from all you good people; this is a hero of the state, a new firm-minded man who has spent years working to—"

Joe's alarm woke him up.

Christ, he said to himself; he sat up groggily. What was that about? Money? Already it had become hazy in his mind. "I made the money," he said aloud, blinking. "Or printed it." Who cares? he said to himself. A dream. Compensation, by the state, for reality. Night after night. It's almost worse than being awake.

No, he decided. *Nothing* is worse than being awake.

He picked up the phone and dialed the bank.

"Interplan Corn and Wheat People's Collective Bank."

"How much are thirty-five thousand crumbles worth in terms of our dollars?" Joe asked.

"Crumbles as in the Plabkian tongue of Sirius five?"

"Right."

"The banking service momentarily was silent and then it said, "$200,000,000,000,000,000,000,000,000,000,000,000, 000,000,000.00."

"Really?" Joe said.

"Would I lie to you?" the bank robot-voice said. "I don't even know who you are."

"Are there any other crumbles?" Joe said. "That is, the word 'crumble' used as a monetary unit in any other enclave, civilization, tribe, cult, or society in the known universe?"

"There is a defunct crumble known several thousand years ago in the—"

"No," Joe said. "This is your active crumble. Thank you and off." He hung up, his ears ringing; he felt as if he had wandered into a titanic auditorium filled with bells of terrible and grand sizes. This must be what they mean by a mystical experience, he said to himself.

His front door opened and two Quietude Civil Authority policemen made their way into the room. As they walked, their keen, frigid glance took in everything inhabiting the room.

"QCA Hymes and Perkin," one of them said as he briefly let Joe see his identification plaque. "You're a pot-healer, Mr. Fernwright; correct? And you're also on the vet-dole; am I right? Yes I'm right," he finished, answering his own question. "What would you say your daily income amounts to, your dole and money received for the alleged work you do?"

The other QCA man pushed open the door of the bathroom. "Something interesting here. The top of the tank, the toilet tank, is off. And he's got a bag of metal coins hanging in there; I should guess about eighty quarters. You're a frugal man, Mr. Fernwright." The QCA man came back into the main room. "How long—"

"Two years," Joe said. "And I'm not breaking any law; I checked with Mr. Attorney before I began."

"What's this about thirty-five thousand Plabkian crumbles?"

Joe hesitated.

It was not an unusual phenomenon, his attitude toward the QCA and their men. They had such neat suits, such good gray and brown weaves. Each carried a briefcase. All looked like highly reputable businessmen—prosperous and responsible, able to make decisions: they were not mere bureaucrats to whom orders were given and who merely carried out orders like pseudorobots . . . and yet they had an inhumanity about them, for no particular reason that he could make out. But then he thought, Ah—I have it. No one could ever imagine a QCA man holding a door open for a lady; that was it; that explained his feeling. A small thing, perhaps, but it seemed to be a comprehension of the severe essence of the QCA throughout. Never hold a door, Joe thought, never take off your hat in an elevator. The ordinary laws of charity did not apply to them, and these laws they did not follow. Ever. But how well shaved they were. How greatly neat.

Strange, he thought, how thinking this could give me the feeling that at last I understand them. But I do. In symbolic form, maybe. But the comprehension is there and it will never go away.

"I got a note," Joe said. "I'll show it to you." He handed them the note which he had found bobbing about in its plastic bottle in the water closet of his facility.

"Who wrote this?" one of the QCA men asked.

"God knows," Joe said.

"Is that a joke?"

Joe said, "You mean is the note a joke, or what I said in answer to your question in saying, 'God knows—' " He broke off, because one of the QCA men was bringing out a teep rod, a receptor which would pick up and record his thoughts for police inspection. "You," Joe said, "will see. That it's true."

The rod, wandlike, hovered over his head for several minutes. No one spoke. Then the QCA man returned the rod to his pocket and stuffed a little speaker into his ear; he played back the tape of Joe's thoughts, listening intently.

"It's so," the QCA man said, and stopped the tape transport, which was located, of course, in his briefcase. "He doesn't know anything about this note, who put it there or why. Sorry, Mr. Fernwright. You know, naturally, that we monitor all phone calls. This one interested us because —as you can probably appreciate—the sum involved is so large."

His companion cop said, "Report to us once a day about this matter." He handed Joe a card. "The number you're to call is on the card. You don't have to ask for anyone in particular; tell whoever answers the call what's developed."

The first QCA man said, "There isn't anything legal that you could do to get paid thirty-five thousand Plabkian crumbles, Mr. Fernwright. It has to be illegal. That's how we see it."

"Maybe there're a hell of a lot of broken pots on Sirius five," Joe said.

"Bit of humor, there," the first QCA man said tartly. He nodded to his companion, and the two of them opened the door and departed from his room. The door closed behind them.

"Maybe it's one gigantic pot," Joe said loudly. "A pot the size of a planet. With fifty glazes and—" He gave up; they probably couldn't hear him anyhow. And originally ornamented by the greatest graphic artist in Plabkian history, he thought. And it's the only product of his genius left, and an earthquake has broken the pot, which is locally worshiped. So the whole Plabkian civilization has collapsed.

Plabkian civilization. Hmm, he thought. Just how far developed are they on Sirius five? he asked himself. A good question.

Going to the phone he dialed the encyclopedia number.

"Good evening," a robotic voice said. "What info do you require, sir or madam?"

Joe said, "Give me a brief description of the social development on Sirius five."

Without the passing of even a tenth second the artificial voice said, "It is an ancient society which has seen better days. The current dominant species on the planet consists of what is called a Glimmung. This shadowy, enormous entity is not native to the planet; it migrated there several centuries ago, taking over from the feeble species such as wubs, werjes, klakes, trobes, and printers left over when the once-ruling master species, the so-called Fog-Things of antiquity, passed away."

"Glimmung—the Glimmung—is all-powerful?" Joe asked.

"His power," the encyclopedia's voice said, "is sharply curtailed by a peculiar book, probably nonexistent, in which, it is alleged, everything which has been, is, and will be, is recorded."

Joe said, "Where did this book come from?"

"You have used up your allotted quantity of information," the voice said. And clicked off.

Joe waited exactly three minutes and then redialed the number.

"Good evening. What info do you require, sir or madam?"

"The book on Sirius five," Joe said. "Which is alleged to tell everything that has been—"

"Oh, it's you again. Well, your trick won't work anymore; we store voice patterns now." It rang off.

That's right, Joe realized. I remember reading in the newspaper about that. It was costing the government too much money the way it was—when we did what I tried to do just now. Nuts, he said to himself. Twenty-four hours before he could get any more free information. Of course, he could go to a private enterprise encyclopedia booth, to Mr. Encyclopedia. But it would cost as much as he had stored in his asbestos bag: the government, when licensing the nonstate-owned enterprises such as Mr. Attorney and Mr. Encyclopedia and Mr. Job, had seen to that.

I think I got aced out, Joe Fernwright said to himself. As usual.

Our society, he thought broodingly, is the perfect form of government. *Everyone* is aced out, in the end.

3

When he reached his work cubicle the next morning he found a second special delivery letter waiting for him.

SHIP OUT TO PLOWMAN'S PLANET, MR. FERNWRIGHT, WHERE YOU ARE NEEDED. YOUR LIFE WILL SIGNIFY SOMETHING; YOU WILL CREATE A PERMANENT ENDEAVOR WHICH WILL OUTLAST ME AS WELL AS YOU.

Plowman's Planet, Joe reflected. It rang a bell, although dimly. Absentmindedly, he dialed the encyclopedia's number.

"Is Plowman's Planet—" he began, but the artificial voice interrupted him.

"Not for another twelve hours. Goodby."

"Just one fact?" he said angrily. "I just want to find out if Sirius five and Plowman's—" Click. The robot mechanism had rung off. Bastards, he thought. All robot servo-mechanisms and all computers are bastards.

Who can I ask? he asked himself, that would know, off-hand, if Plowman's Planet is Sirius five? Kate. Kate would know.

But, he thought as he started to dial her office number, if I'm going to emigrate to Plowman's Planet I don't want her to know; she'll be able to trace me re my back alimony payments.

Once more he picked up the unsigned note, studied it. And, in a gradual, seeping fashion, a realization concerning it suffused his mind and entered into his field of awareness. There were more words on the note in some kind of semi-invisible ink. Runic writing? he wondered; he felt a sort of wicked, animal excitement, as if he had found a carefully protected trail.

He dialed Smith's number. "If you got a letter," Joe said, "with semi-invisible runic writing on it, how would you— you in particular—go about making it visible?"

"I'd hold it over a heat source," Smith said.

"Why?" Joe said.

"Because it's most likely written in milk. And writing in milk turns black over a heat source."

"Runic writing in *milk?*" Joe said angrily.

"Statistics show—"

"I can't imagine it. I simply can't imagine it. Runic writing in milk." He shook his head. "Anyway, what statistics are there on runic writing? This is absurd." He got out his cigarette lighter and held it beneath the sheet of paper. At once, black letters became visible.

WE SHALL RAISE HELDSCALLA.

"What's it say?" Smith asked.

Joe said, "Listen, Smith; you haven't used the encyclopedia in the last twenty-four hours, have you?"

"No," Smith said.

Joe said, "Call it. Ask it if Plowman's Planet is another name for Sirius five. And ask it what 'Heldscalla' consists of." I guess I could ask the dictionary that, he said to himself. "What a mess," he said. "Is this any way to conduct business?" He felt fear overlaid with nausea; it did not appeal to him. It did not seem effective nor funny; it was merely strange. And, he thought, I have to report this to the police, so I'll be back cloistered with them again, and now there's probably already a file on me—hell, he thought, there has been since my birth—but now the file has new entries. Which always was bad. As every citizen knew.

Heldscalla, he thought. An odd and somehow impressive verbal integer. It appealed to him; it seemed totally opposed to such conditions as cubicles, phones, walking to work through endless crowds, fiddling his life away on the veterans' dole, meanwhile playing The Game. I am here, he thought, when I should be there.

"Call me back, Smith," he said into the phone. "As soon as you've talked to the encyclopedia. Bye." He rang off, paused, then dialed the dictionary. "Heldscalla," he said. "What does it mean?"

The dictionary—or rather its artificial voice—said, "Heldscalla is the ancient cathedral of the once-ruling Fog-Things of Sirius five. It sank under the sea centuries ago and has never been placed back, intact and functioning, with its old, holy artifacts and relics, on dry land."

"Are you hooked into the encyclopedia right now?" Joe asked. "That's an awful lot of definition."

"Yes, sir or madam; I am hooked into the encyclopedia."

"Then can you tell me any more?"

"No more."

"Thank you," Joe Fernwright said huskily. And hung up.

He could see it. Glimmung—or *the* Glimmung, if that was correct; evidently there was only one of them—intended to raise the ancient cathedral Heldscalla, and to do so, the Glimmung needed a wide span of skills. Such as his own, for example; his ability to heal ceramic ware. Heldscalla obviously contained pots—enough of them to cause the Glimmung to approach him . . . and to offer him a good sum for his work.

By now he's probably recruited two hundred skills from two hundred planets, Joe realized. I'm not the only one getting peculiar letters et cetera. He saw in his mind a great cannon being fired, and out of it special delivery letters, thousands of them, addressed to various life-form individuals throughout the galaxy.

And oh god, he thought. The police are spotting it; they barged into my room minutes after I consulted the bank. Last night, those two; they knew already what these letters and weird note floating in the water closet of the toilet mean. They could have told me. But of course they wouldn't; that would be too natural, too humane.

His phone buzzed. He lifted the receiver.

"I contacted the encyclopedia," Smith said, as his image appeared on the screen. "Plowman's Planet is space argot for Sirius five. Since I had hold of the encyclopedia I took the opportunity of asking it more. I thought you might appreciate it."

"Yes," Joe said.

"One vast old creature lives there. Apparently infirm."

"You mean it's sick?" Joe asked.

"Well, you know . . . age and such like. Dormant; that's what it's been."

"Is it menacing?"

"How could it be menacing if it's dormant as well as infirm? It's senile. Yes, that's the word—senile."

Joe asked, "Has it ever said anything?"

"Not really."

"Not even the time of day?"

"Ten years ago it came to briefly and asked for an orbiting weather-station satellite."

"What did it pay for it with?"

"It didn't. It's indigent. We contributed it free, and we

threw in a news type satellite along with the weather one.''

"Broke and senile," Joe said. He felt glum. "Well," he said, "I guess I won't be getting any money out of it."

"Why? Were you suing it?"

"Goodby, Smith," Joe said.

"Wait!" Smith said. "There's a new game. You want to join? It consists of speed-scanning the newspaper archives to come up with the funniest headline. *Real* headline, you realize; not made up. I have a good one; it's from 1962. You want to hear it?"

"Okay," Joe said, still feeling glum. His glumness had oozed throughout him, leaving him inert and spongelike; he responded reflexively. "Let's hear your headline."

"ELMO PLASKETT SINKS GIANTS," Smith read from his slip of paper.

"Who the hell was Elmo Plaskett?"

"He came up from the minors and—"

"I have to go, now," Joe said, standing up. "I have to leave my office." He hung up. Home, he said to himself. To get my bag of quarters.

4

Along the sidewalks of the city the vast animallike gasping entity which was the mass of Cleveland's unemployed—and unemployable—gathered and stood, stood and waited, waited and fused together into a lump both unstable and sad. Joe Fernwright, carrying his sack of coins, rubbed against their collective flank as he pushed his way toward the corner and the Mr. Job booth. He smelled the familiar vinegarlike penetrating scent of their presence, their overheated and yet plaintively disappointed massiveness. On all sides of him their eyes contemplated his forward motion, his determination to get past them.

"Excuse me," he said to a slender Mexican-looking youth who had become wedged, among all the others, directly ahead of him.

The youth blinked nervously, but did not move. He had seen the asbestos bag which Joe held; beyond any doubt he knew what Joe had and where Joe was going and what Joe intended to do.

"Can I get by?" Joe asked him. It seemed an impasse of permanent proportions. Behind him, the throng of inactive humanity had closed in, blocking any chance of retreat. He could not go back and he could make no progress forward. I guess the next thing, he thought, is that they'll grab my quarters and that will be that. His heart hurt, as if he had climbed a ridge, a final ridge of life itself, a terrible hill strewn with skulls. He saw, about him, gaping eye sockets; he experienced a weird visual distortion, as if the ultimate disposition of these people had made its appearance palpably . . . as if, he thought, it can't wait; it must have them now.

The Mexican youth said, "Could I look at your coins, sir?"

It was hard to know what to do. The eyes—or rather the hollow sockets—continued to press in at him in a complete circle; he felt them encompass him and his asbestos bag. I am shrinking, he thought in surprise. Why? He felt weak and glum, but not guilty. It was his money. They knew it and he knew it. And yet the vacant eyes made him small. As if, he thought, it doesn't matter what I do, whether I get to the Mr. Job booth or not; what I do, what becomes of me—it won't change things for these people.

And yet, on a conscious level, he didn't care. They had their lives; he had his, and his included a sack of carefully saved-up metal coins. Can they contaminate me? he asked himself. Drag me down into their inertial storm? This is their problem, not mine, he thought. I'm not going to sink with the system; this is my first decision, to ignore the two special delivery letters and do this: take this journey with this sack of quarters. This is the start of my escape, and there will be no new bondage.

"No," he said.

"I won't take any," the youth said.

A strange impulse overcame Joe Fernwright. Opening the bag he rummaged, got out a quarter; he held it out toward the Mexican youth. As the boy accepted it other hands appeared, on all sides; the ring of hopeless eyes had become a ring of outstretched, open hands. But there was no greed conspiring against him; none of the hands tried to grab his sack of coins. The hands were simply there, merely waiting. Waiting in a silence made up of trust, as his own earlier waiting at the mail tube had been. Horrible, Joe thought. These people think I'm going to give them a present, as if they've been waiting for the universe to do this: the universe has given them nothing all their lives and they have accepted that as silently as now. They see me as a kind of supernatural deity. But no, he thought. I've got to get out of here. I can't do anything for them.

But even as he realized this he found himself digging into the cloth sack; he found himself putting a quarter into one palm after another.

Overhead, a police cruiser whistled loudly as it lowered, like a great lid, its two occupants in their slick, bright uniforms, wearing riot helmets that sparkled, holding, each of them, a laser rifle. One of the two cops said, "Get out of this man's way."

The pressing circle began to melt back. The extended hands disappeared, as if into a numbed, intolerable darkness.

"Don't stand there," the other cop said to Joe in his thick cop's voice. "Get moving. Get those coins out of here or I'll write you out a citation after which you won't have one goddam coin left."

Joe walked on.

"What do you think you are?" the other cop said to him, as the cruiser followed after him, holding its position directly above his head. "Some sort of privately endowed philanthropic organization?"

Saying nothing, Joe continued on.

"You're required by law to answer me," the cop said.

Reaching into his asbestos cloth sack, Joe got out a quarter. He handed it up toward the nearer of the two cops. And, at the same time, saw with amazement that only a few quarters remained.

My coins, he realized, are gone! So there is only one door

open to me—the mail tube and what it has brought in the last two days. Whether I like it or not—by what I've done just now it's been decided.

"Why did you hand me this coin?" the cop asked.

"As a tip," Joe said. And, at the same time, felt his head burst as the laser beam, on stun, hit him directly between his eyes.

At the police station the swank young police official, blond-haired, blue-eyed, slim, in his swank clean uniform, said, "We're not going to book you, Mr. Fernwright, although technically you're guilty of a crime against the people."

"The state," Joe said; he sat hunched over, rubbing his forehead, trying to make the pain stop. "Not the people," he managed to say. He shut his eyes and the pain flooded over him, radiating out from the spot where the beam had touched him.

"What you're saying," the young police official said, "con-stitutes in itself a felony and we could book you on that, too. We could even turn you over to the Political Control Bureau as an enemy of the working class, engaged in a conspiracy to advocate agitation against the people and the servants of the people, such as ourselves. But your record heretofore—" He studied Joe with professional intensity. "A sane man doesn't start handing coins out to total strangers." The police official examined a document which had come unreeling itself out of a slot of his desk. "Obviously you acted without de-liberation."

"Yes," Joe said. "Without deliberation." He felt nothing in the way of emotions; he experienced only bodily discom-fort, acute and still growing. It had preempted any feeling, any mental activity.

"However, we're going to impound your remaining coins. For the present at least. And you'll be on probation for a year, during which time you will report here, once a week, and give us an account, a full account, of your activities."

"Without a trial?" Joe said.

"Do you want to be tried?" the police official eyed him keenly.

"No," Joe said. He went on rubbing his head. The QCA material apparently hasn't been fed to their computers yet, he decided. But eventually it'll all be combined. They'll put it all together, my tipping the cop, my finding notes in the water closet of my toilet. I'm a nut, he said to himself. I've gone mad from inactivity; the last seven months have destroyed me. And now, when I made my move, when I took my coins to Mr. Job—*I couldn't do it.*

"Wait a minute," another cop said. "Here's something on him from QCA. It just rolled down the circuit from their computer bank central."

Turning, Joe ran toward the door of the police station. Toward the mass of people outside. As if to bury himself among them; to cease to be a finite part.

Two cops appeared ahead of him and they lunged toward him as he ran; they came closer unnaturally rapidly, as if on video tape speeded up. And then, suddenly, they were under water; they, like slender silver fish, gaped at him and rhythmically maneuvered themselves among—good god! coral and seaweed. And yet he himself felt nothing, no water; but here was a tank of water, instead of the police station, all the furniture like sunken wrecks, half-buried in sand. And the police twisted and streaked by him, lovely in their glittering gliding movements. But they could not touch him, because he, although standing in the center, was not in the tank. And he heard no sound. Their mouths moved, but only silence reached him.

Bobbing and undulating, a squid swept past him; it was, he thought, like the soul of the sea. The squid all at once ejected clouds of darkness, as if meant to efface everything. He saw no police officers, now; the darkness propagated itself until it filled up the panorama and then it became more intense, as if it were not opaque enough before. But I can breathe, Joe said. "Hey," he said aloud—and heard his own voice. I'm just not in the water, he realized, like they are. I can identify myself; I'm split off, a separate entity. But why?

What if I try to move? he wondered. He took one step, another, and then clunk; he rebounded off a wall-like surface. Another way, he said; he turned and took a step to his right. Clunk. In panic he thought, I'm in a box like a coffin! Did they kill me? he asked himself. When I tried to run for the door. He reached his arms out, into the darkness, groping . . . and something was placed in his right hand. Small, square. With two disklike knobs.

A transistor radio.

He turned it on.

"Hi there, folks!" a happy, tinny voice sounded in the darkness. "This is Cavorting Cary Karns here with six phones sitting in front of me and twenty switchboard circuits going, so that I can hear you all, all of you good people who want to discuss something, anything. The number is 394-950-911111, so call in, folks, about anything at all, whatever's on your mind, good, bad, indifferent, interesting, or dull—just call Cavorting Cary Karns at 394-950-911111 and the whole radio audience out there will hear you and what you have to say, your opinion, a fact that you know that you think everyone else should know—" From the speaker of the transistor radio came the sound of a phone ringing. "Hello—we've got a caller already!" Cavorting Cary Karns declared. "Yes sir. Yes ma'am, I mean."

"Mr. Karns," a shrill female voice said, "there ought to be a stop sign placed at the intersection of Fulton Avenue and Clover, where all the little schoolchildren, and I see them every day—"

Something hard, some dense object, bumped Joe's left hand. He took hold of it. A phone.

Sitting down, he placed the phone and the transistor radio in front of him and then he got out his cigarette lighter and zipped the butane flame on. It illuminated a meager circle, but within the circle he could make out the phone and the transistor radio. A Zenith transistor radio, he noted. Evidently a good one, from the size of it.

"Okay, folks out there," Cavorting Cary Karns merrily prattled. "The number is 394-950-911111; that's where you'll reach me and through me the whole world of—"

Joe dialed. At last he had painstakingly dialed the whole number. He held the receiver to his ear, listened to a busy signal for a moment, and then heard, from both the receiver and the radio, the voice of Cavorting Cary Karns. "Yes sir, or is it ma'am?" Karns asked.

"Where am I?" Joe said into the phone.

"Hey there!" Karns said. "We've got somebody out there, some poor soul, who's lost. Your name is, sir?"

"Joseph Fernwright," Joe said.

"Well, Mr. Fernwright, it's a downright pleasure to talk to you. Your question is, Where are you? Does anybody know where Mr. Joseph Fernwright of Cleveland—you are in Cleveland, aren't you, Mr. Fernwright?—does anybody out there know where he is, at this moment? I think this is a valid question on Mr. Fernwright's part; I'd like to hold the lines open for anyone who can call in and give us some idea, at least a general idea, of the vicinity in which Mr. Fernwright is currently. So you other people, who don't know where Mr. Fernwright is, could you not call in until we've located Mr. Fernwright? Mr. Fernwright, it shouldn't be long; we've got a ten million audience and a fifty-thousand-watt transmitter going and—wait! A call." Tinny sound of a phone ringing. "Yes sir or ma'am. Sir. Your name, sir?"

A male voice, from the radio and from Joe's phone, said, "My name is Dwight L. Glimmung of 301 Pleasant Hill Road, and I know where Mr. Fernwright is. He's in my basement. Slightly to the right and a little behind my furnace. He's in a wooden packing crate that came with an air-conditioning unit that I ordered from People's Sears, last year."

"You hear that, Mr. Fernwright?" Cavorting Cary Karns

whooped. "You're in a packing crate in Mr. Dwight L.—what was the rest of your name, sir?"

"Glimmung."

"Mr. Dwight L. Glimmung's basement of 301 Pleasant Hill Road. So all your troubles are over, Mr. Fernwright. Simply get out of the packing crate and you'll be just fine!"

"I don't want him to bust the crate, though," Dwight L. Glimmung said. "Maybe I better go down there into that basement and pry a few boards loose and let him out."

"Mr. Fernwright," Karns said, "just for the edification of our radio audience, how did you happen to get into an empty packing crate in the basement of Mr. Dwight L. Glimmung of 301 Pleasant Hill Road? I'm sure our audience would like to know."

"I don't know," Joe said.

"Well, perhaps then Mr. Glimmung—Mr. Glimmung? He seems to have rung off. Evidently he's on his way down into the basement to let you out, Mr. Fernwright. What a lucky thing for you it was, sir, that Mr. Glimmung happened to be listening to this show! Otherwise you probably would be in that crate until doomsday. And now let's turn to another listener; hello?" The phone clicked in Joe's ear. The circuit had been broken.

Sounds. From around him. A creaking noise and something wide bent back; light flooded into the box wherein Joe Fernwright sat with his cigarette lighter, his phone, and his transistor radio.

"I got you out of the police barracks the best way I could," a male voice—the same that Joe had heard on the radio—said.

"A strange way," Joe said.

"To you strange. Strange to me have been a number of things you've done since the time I first became aware of you."

Joe said, "Like giving away my coins."

"No, I understood that. What strikes me as odd is your

having sat for all those months in your work cubicle, waiting."
A second slat slid away; more light flooded in at Joe and he
blinked. He tried to see Glimmung, but he still could not.
"Why didn't you go to a nearby museum and break a number
of their pots anonymously . . . and you would have got their
business. And the pots would be healed as new. Nothing
would have been lost and you would have been active and
productive over these days." The last slat fell away, and Joe
Fernwright saw, up in the full light, the creature from Sirius
five, the life-form which the encyclopedia had described as
being senile and penniless.

He saw a great hoop of water spinning on a horizonal axis,
and, within it, on a vertical axis, a transversal hoop of fire.
Hanging over and behind the two elemental hoops a curtain
draped and floated, a billowing fabric which he saw, with
amazement, was Paisley.

And—one more aspect: an image embedded at the nucleus
of the revolving hoops of fire and water. The pleasant, pretty
face of a brown-haired teen-age girl. It hung suspended, and
it smiled at him . . . an ordinary face, easily forgotten but
always encountered. It was, he thought, a composite mask,
as if drawn on a blank sidewalk with colored chalk. A temporary and not very impressive visage, through which Glimmung apparently meant to encounter him. But the hoop of
water, he thought. The basis of the universe. As was the hoop
of fire. And they revolved on and on, at a perfectly regulated
speed. A superb and eternal self-perpetuating mechanism,
he thought, except for the flimsy Paisley shawl and the im-
mature female face. He felt bewildered. Did what he see add
up to strength? Certainly it gave no aura of senility, and yet
he had the impression that, despite the jejune face, it was
very old. As to its financial status, he could make no estimate
at this time. That would have to come later, if at all.

"I bought this house seven years ago," Glimmung—or at
least a voice—said. "When there was a buyers' market."

Joe, looking for the source of the voice, distinguished an

oddity which twitched his blood and made him cold, as if ice and fire had mixed together in him, a pale analog of Glimmung.

The voice. It came from an ancient wind-up Victrola, on which a record played at a peculiar high speed. Glimmung's voice was on the record.

"Yeah, I guess you're right," Joe said. "Seven years ago was a good time to buy. You do your recruiting from here?"

"I work here," Glimmung's voice—from the ancient wind-up Victrola—answered. "I work many other places as well . . . in many star systems. Now let me tell you where you stand, Joe Fernwright. To the police you simply turned and walked out of the building, and for some reason they seemed unable, at the time, to stop you. But an APB has been sent out regarding you, so you can't go back to your rooming house or your work cubicle."

"Without being caught by the police," Joe said.

"Do you want that?"

"Maybe it has to be," Joe said stoically.

"Nonsense. Your police are feral and malicious. I want you to see Heldscalla, as it was before it sank. Youuuuuuuuu," and the phonograph ran down. Joe, via the handcrank, wound it up again, feeling a mixture of feelings, each of which he would probably, if asked, be unable to describe. "You will find a viewing instrument on the table to your right," Glimmung said, the record now playing at its proper speed. "A depth-perception mechanism originating here on your own planet."

Joe searched—and found an antique stereoscope viewer, circa 1900, with a set of black-and-white cards to be put into it. "Couldn't you do better than this?" he demanded. "A film sequence, or stereo video tape. Why, this thing was invented before the automobile." It came to him, then. "You are broke," he said. "Smith was right."

"That's a calumny," Glimmung said. "I am merely parsimonious. It is an inherited characteristic of my order. As a product of your socialistic society you are used to great waste. I, however, am still on the free enterprise plan. 'A penny saved—' "

"Oh Christ," Joe groaned.

"If you want me to quit," Glimmung said, "merely lift the mica-disk playback head-and-needle assembly from the record."

"What happens when the record comes to an end?" Joe said.

"It will never do so."

"Then it's not a real record."

"It's a real record. The grooves form a loop."

"What do you really look like?" Joe said.

Glimmung said, "What do *you* really look like?"

Nettled, Joe said, gesticulating, "It depends on whether you accept Kant's division of phenomena from the *Ding an sich,* the thing in itself which like Leibnitz's windowless monad—"

He halted, because the phonograph had run down again; the record had ceased to turn. As he rewound it, Joe thought, He probably didn't hear anything I said. And probably on purpose.

"I missed your philosophical discourse," the phonograph declared, when he had finished rewinding it.

"What I'm saying," Joe said, "is that a phenomenon perceived is done so in the structural percept-system of the perceiver. Much of what you see in perceiving me—" He pointed to himself for emphasis. "—is a projection from your own mind. To another percept-system I would appear quite different. To the police, for instance. There're as many world-views as there are sentient creatures."

"Hmm," Glimmung said.

"You understand the distinction I'm making," Joe said.

"Mr. Fernwright, what do you really want? The time has come for you to choose, to act. To participate—or not participate—in a great historical moment. At this moment, Mr.

Fernwright, I am in a thousand places, committing or helping to commit an enormous variety of engineers and artisans . . . you are one craftsman out of many. I can't wait for you any longer."

"Am I vital to the project?" Joe asked.

"A pot-healer is vital, yes. You or someone else."

Joe said, "When do I get my thirty-five thousand crumbles? In advance?"

"You will get them whennnnnn," Glimmung began to say, but again the old Victrola became unwound; the record slowed to a halt.

Cagey bastard, Joe said to himself grimly as he rewound the phonograph.

"When," Glimmung said, "and if, only if, the cathedral is raised once more as it was centuries ago."

That's what I thought, Joe thought.

"Will you go to Plowman's Planet?" Glimmung asked.

For a time Joe considered. In his mind he considered his room, the cubicle in which he worked, the loss of his coins, the police—he thought about it all and tried to make it add up. What ties me here? he asked himself. The known, he decided. The fact that I am used to it. You can get used to anything, and even learn to like it. Pavlov's theory of learned reflex is correct; I am held by habit. And nothing more.

"Could I have just a few crumbles in advance?" he asked Glimmung. "I want to buy a cashmere sports jacket and a new pair of wash-and-wear shoes."

The phonograph split apart; pieces of it rained everywhere, lancing Joe's arms and face. And, in the center of the hoops of water and of fire, a huge contorted furious face manifested itself; the feeble female countenance disappeared, and what glared at Joe now glared with the force of a sun. The face cursed at him, cursed in a language he did not know. He shrank back, appalled by the anger of Glimmung; the ordinary objects through which Glimmung had up to now manifested himself disintegrated into bits, the Paisley shawl, even the two elemental hoops. The basement itself began to crack apart, like a declining ruin; pieces of cement fell to the floor and then the floor itself broke like dried clay.

Jesus, Joe thought. And Smith said it was senile. Now huge chunks of the house were dropping around him; a section of pipe banged him on the head and he heard a thousand voices singing a thousand songs of fear. "I'll go," he said aloud, his eyes shut, hands enwrapping his head. "You're right; it's not a joke. I'm sorry. I know this has great importance to you."

The fist of Glimmung clutched him around the waist; it lifted him up as it squeezed him like a roll of newspaper. He saw for an instant the raging, melting, burning eye—a single eye!—and then the firestorm ebbed. The pressure around his waist relaxed, just a trifle. But enough. He thought, I probably didn't get any ribs cracked. I better get a medical examination before I leave Earth, though. Just to be sure.

"I will set you down in the main lounge of the Cleveland Spaceport," Glimmung said. "You will find that you have enough money for a ticket to Plowman's Planet. Take the next flight; do not go back to your room for your things—the police are waiting for you there. Take this." Glimmung thrust something into his hand; in the light it reflected many colors; the colors blended into one shape and then trickled out in threadlike streams to re-form in another pattern. And then another, which leaped up at him wildly.

"A potsherd," Glimmung said.

"This is a piece of a broken vase of the cathedral?" Joe said. "Why didn't you show it to me right away?" I would have gone, he thought, if I had seen this . . . if I had had any idea.

"Now you know," Glimmung said, "what you will be healing with your talent."

5

A man is an angel that has become deranged, Joe Fernwright
thought. Once they—all of them—had been genuine angels,
and at that time they had had a choice between good and
evil, so it was easy, easy being an angel. And then something
happened. Something went wrong or broke down or failed.
And they had become faced with the necessity of choosing
not good or evil but the lesser of two evils, and so that had
unhinged them and now each was a man.

Seated on the plush plastic bench at the Cleveland Spaceport, waiting for his flight, Joe felt weak and unsure of himself, and ahead of him lay a terrible job—terrible in the sense
that it would put inordinate demands on his waning strength.
I am like a gray thing, he thought. Bustling along with the
currents of air that tumble me, that roll me, like a gray puff-
ball, on and on.

Strength. The strength of being, he thought, and opposite
to that the peace of nonbeing. Which was better? Strength
wore out in the end, every time; so perhaps that was the
answer and no more was needed. Strength—being—was temporary. And peace—nonbeing—was eternal; it had existed

prior to his birth and would resume for him after his death. The period of strength, in between, was merely an episode, a short flexing of borrowed muscles—a body which would have to be returned . . . to the real owner.

Had he not met Glimmung he would never have thought this—realized it. But in Glimmung he witnessed eternal, self-renewing strength. Glimmung, like a star, fed on himself, and was never consumed. And, like a star, he was beautiful; he was a fountain, a meadow, an empty twilight street over which dwelt a fading sky. The sky would fade; the twilight would become darkness, but Glimmung would blaze on, as if burning out the impurities of everyone and everything around him. He was the light who exposed the soul and all its decayed parts. And, with that light, he scorched out of existence those decayed portions, here and there: mementos of a life not asked for.

Seated there in the waiting room of the spaceport, seated upon the unpleasant plastic chair, Joe heard rocket motors winding up. He turned his head, saw through the great window an LB-4 rise upward, shaking the building and everything in it. And then, in a matter of seconds, it had gone; nothing remained.

I gaze across the silence of the marshes, he thought, and out of them, mysterious and wild, pops the sound of giant vehicles.

Getting to his feet he crossed the waiting room to the Padre booth; seated inside he put a dime into the slot and dialed at random. The marker came to rest at Zen.

"Tell me your torments," the Padre said, in an elderly voice marked with compassion. And slowly; it spoke as if there were no rush, no pressure. All was timeless.

Joe said, "I haven't worked for seven months and now I've got a job that takes me out of the Sol System entirely, and I'm afraid. What if I can't do it? What if after so long I've lost my skill?"

The Padre's weightless voice floated reassuringly back to

him. "You have worked and not worked. Not working is the hardest work of all."

That's what I get for dialing Zen, Joe said to himself. Before the Padre could intone further he switched to Puritan Ethic.

"Without work," the Padre said, in a somewhat more forceful voice, "a man is nothing. He ceases to exist."

Rapidly, Joe dialed Roman Catholic.

"God and God's love will accept you," the Padre said in a faraway gentle voice. "You are safe in His arms. He will never—"

Joe dialed Allah.

"Kill your foe," the Padre said.

"I have no foe," Joe said. "Except for my own weariness and fear of failure."

"Those are enemies," the Padre said, "which you must overcome in a *jihad;* you must show yourself to be a man, and a man, a true man, is a fighter who fights back." The Padre's voice was stern.

Joe dialed Judaism.

"A bowl of Martian fatworm soup—" the Padre began soothingly, but then Joe's money wore out; the Padre closed down, inert and dead—or anyhow dormant.

Fatworm soup, Joe reflected. The most nourishing food known. Maybe that's the best advice of all, he thought. I'll head for the spaceport's restaurant.

There, on a stool, he seated himself and picked up the menu.

"Care for a tobacco cigarette?" the man next to him said.

Horrified, Joe stared at him and said, "My god—you can't smoke a cigarette out in the open—especially here." He turned toward the man in agitation; he started to speak on. And then he realized whom he was speaking to.

In human form Glimmung sat beside him.

• • •

"I never intended," Glimmung said, "for you to be so troubled. Your work is good; I've told you that. I picked you because I consider you the finest pot-healer on Earth; I've told you that, too. The Padre was right; you need something to eat and a chance to calm down. I'll order for you." Glimmung nodded to the robot mechanism from which the food came—nodded as he openly smoked his tobacco cigarette.

"Can't they see the cigarette?" Joe asked.

"No," Glimmung said. "And evidently the food-dispensing mechanism can't see me either." Turning toward Joe he said, "You order."

After he had eaten his bowl of fatworm soup and had drunk his caffeine-free (it had to be so, by law) coffee, Joe said, "I don't think you understand. To someone like you—"

"What am I like?" Glimmung said.

"Don't you know?" Joe said.

"No creature knows itself," Glimmung said. "You don't know yourself; you don't have any knowledge, none at all, of your most basic potentials. Do you understand what the Raising will mean for you? Everything that has been latent, has been potential, in you—all of it will become actualized. Everyone who conspires in the Raising, everyone involved, from a hundred planets tossed here and there in the galaxy— everyone will *be*. You have never been, Joe Fernwright. You merely exist. To be is to do. And we will do a great thing, Joe Fernwright." Glimmung's voice rang like steel.

"Did you come here to talk me out of my doubts?" Joe asked. "Is that why you're at the spaceport? To make sure I don't change my mind and drop out at the last moment?" It couldn't be that; he was not that important. Glimmung, stretched between fifteen worlds, would not be lowering himself to this, to an attempt to restore the confidence of one meager pot-healer from Cleveland; Glimmung had too much to do: there were larger matters.

Glimmung said, "This is a 'larger matter.' "

"Why?"

"Because there are no small matters. Just as there is no small life. The life of an insect, a spider; his life is as large as yours, and yours is as large as mine. Life is life. You wish to live as much as I do; you have spent seven months of hell, waiting day after day for what you needed . . . the way a spider waits. Think about the spider, Joe Fernwright. He makes his web. Then he makes a little silk cave at the end of the web to sit in. He holds strands that lead to every part of the web, so that he will know when something to eat, something he must have to live, arrives. He waits. A day goes by. Two days. A week. He waits on; there is nothing he can do but wait. The little fisherman of the night . . . and perhaps something comes, and he lives, or nothing comes, and he waits and he thinks, 'It won't come in time. It is too late.' And he is right; he dies still waiting."

"But for me," Joe said, "something came in time."

"I came," Glimmung said.

Joe said, "Did you pick me because of—" He hesitated. "Out of pity?"

"Never," Glimmung said. "The Raising will take great skill, many skills, many knowings and crafts, vast numbers of arts. Do you still have that potsherd with you?"

Joe got the small divine fragment from his coat pocket; he put it down on the lunch counter, beside the empty bowl of soup.

"Thousands of them," Glimmung said. "You have, I should guess, a hundred more years of life. It can't be done in a hundred years; you will step among them, the beautiful little pieces, until the day you die. And you will get your wish; you will *be*, until the end. And, having been, you will always exist." Glimmung looked at the Omega wristwatch that circled his humanoid wrist. "They will be announcing your flight in two minutes."

After he had been strapped to his couch, and the pressure

helmet had been screwed over his head, he managed to twist around so that he could hopefully see his flight companion, the person beside him.

Mali Yojez, the tag read. He squinted and saw that it was a girl, non-Terran but humanoid.

And then the first thrust rockets ignited and the ship began to rise.

He had never been off Earth before, and he realized this starkly as the weight on him grew. This—is—not—like—going—from—New York—to Tokyo, he said to himself gaspingly. With incalculable effort he managed to turn his head so that he could once again see the non-Terran girl. She had become blue. Maybe it's natural to her race, Joe thought. Maybe I've turned blue, too. Maybe I'm dying, he said to himself, and then the booster rockets came on . . . and Joe Fernwright passed out.

When he awoke he heard only the sound of the Mahler "Fourth" and a low murmur of voices. I'm the last to come out of it, he said to himself gloomily. The pert, dark-haired stewardess busily unscrewed his pressure helmet and shut off his separate supply of oxygen.

"Feeling better, Mr. Fernwright?" the stewardess inquired as she delicately recombed his hair. "Miss Yojez has been reading the biographical material you gave us before flight-time, and she is very interested in meeting you. There; now your hair looks just ever so fine. Don't you think so, Miss Yojez?"

"How do you do, Mr. Fernwright?" Miss Yojez asked him in a heavily accented voice. "I have been glad to know you very. In the lengthitude of our trip I am surprised not to talk to you, because I think we in common much have."

"May I see Miss Yojez's biographical material?" Joe asked the stewardess; it was handed to him and he scanned it rapidly. Favorite animal: a squimp. Favorite color: rej. Favorite game: Monopoly. Favorite music: koto, classical and Kimio

Eto. Born in the Prox system, which made her a pioneer, of sorts.

"I think," Miss Yojez said, "we are in the same undertaking, several of us with the inclusion of I and me."

"You and me," Joe said.

"You're natural Earth?"

"I've never been off Earth in my life," Joe said.

"Then this is your first space flight."

"Yes," he said. He eyed her covertly and found her attractive; her short-clipped bronze hair formed an effective contrast to her light gray skin. In addition, she had one of the smallest waists he had ever seen, and in the permo-form spray-foam blouse and pants this as well as the rest of her stood cleanly revealed. "You're a marine biologist," he said, reading more of her biographical material.

"Indeed. I am to determine the depth of coral investation of—" She paused, brought forth a small dictionary and looked up a word. "Submerged artifacts."

He felt curiosity toward one point; he asked, "How did Glimmung manifest himself to you?"

" 'Manifest,' " Miss Yojez echoed; she searched through her small dictionary.

"Materializing," the stewardess said brightly. "There is a circuit of the ship linking us with a translation computer back on Earth. At each couch is an earphone and microphone. Here are yours, Mr. Fernwright, and here are yours, Miss Yojez."

"My Terran linguistic skills are returning," Miss Yojez said, rejecting the earphone. To Joe she said, "What did you—"

"How did Glimmung appear to you?" Joe asked. "Physically what did he look like? Big? Short? Portly?"

Miss Yojez said, "Glimmung initially manifests himself in an aquatic framework, inasmuch as he, proper, often rests at the bottom of the oceans of his planet, in the—" She culled her mind. "The vicinity of the sunken cathedral."

That explained the oceanic transformation at the police

station. "But subsequently how did he appear?" he asked. "The same?"

"The second time he came to I," Miss Yojez said, "he manifested himself as a laundry of basket."

Can she mean that? Joe wondered. A basket of laundry? He thought, then, of The Game; the old preoccupation abruptly stirred into life inside him. "Miss Yojez," he said, "perhaps we could make use of the computer translator . . . they can be very interesting. Let me tell you about an incident that occurred in automated translating of a Soviet article on engineering years ago. The term—"

"Please," Miss Yojez said, "I can't follow you and additionally we have things other to discuss. We must ask everyone and find out how many has been employed by Mr. Glimmung." She fitted the earphone to the side of her head, lifted the microphone and pressed all the buttons on the translation console beside her. "Would everyone who is going to Plowman's Planet to work in Mr. Glimmung's undertaking raise their hands, please?"

"So anyway," Joe said, "this article on engineering, when the computer translated it into English, had one strange term in it that appeared over and over. 'Water sheep.' What the hell does that mean? they all asked. I dunno, they all said. Well, what finally they—"

Miss Yojez broke in, "Of the forty-five of us aboard this ship thirty are in Glimmung's pay." She laughed. "Perhaps now is the time for us to establish a union and work collectively."

A stern-looking gray-haired man at the front end of the section said, "That's not a half bad idea, actually."

"But he's already paying so much," a timid little fellow on the left side pointed out.

"Is it in writing?" the gray-haired man said. "He's made oral promises to us and then he's threatened us, or at least so I gather. Anyhow he threatened me. He came on like the day of judgment; it really took the wind out of my sails, and if you knew me you'd know it's rare when anyone can do that to Harper Baldwin."

"So anyhow," Joe said, "they finally managed to trace it back to the original paper, in Russian, and you know what it was? It was 'hydraulic ram.' And it came out in English as 'water sheep.' Now, on the basis of this, I and a number of distinguished colleagues—"

"Oral promises," a sharp-faced middle-aged woman toward the rear of the section said, "are not enough. Before we do any work for him we should have written contracts. Basically, when you get down to it, he's gotten us on this ship by intimidation."

"Then think what a threat he'll be when we get to Plowman's Planet," Miss Yojez pointed out.

All the passengers were silent for a moment.

"We just call it The Game," Joe said.

"In addition," the gray-haired man said, "we must remember that we're only a small part of the work force that Glimmung's been recruiting all over the galaxy. I mean, we can act collective to hell and gone, and what does it matter? We're just a drop in the bucket, we here. Or eventually we'll be, when he gets the others onto his damn planet, which could be any time."

"What we'll have to do," Miss Yojez said, "is to organize ourselves here, and then, when we reach Plowman's Planet, we'll probably be staying at one of the major hotels, and once there we can contact some or all of the others he's recruited and then possibly we can form a union effective."

A heavyset red-faced man said, "But isn't Glimmung a—" He gestured. "A supernatural creature? A deity?"

"There are no deities," the timid little fellow on the left side of the compartment said. "I used to put strong faith in them at an earlier age of my life, but after keen and very recurrent frustration and disappointment and disillusionment I gave up."

The red-faced man said, "In terms of what he can do.

What does it matter what you call it?" Vigorously, he declared, "In relation to us, Glimmung has the power and nature of a deity. For example, he can manifest himself simultaneously on ten or fifteen planets all over the galaxy, and yet still remain on Plowman's Planet. Yes, he manifested himself to me in a scary fashion, as that gentleman up front just pointed out. But I'm convinced it's the real thing. Glimmung *made* us come here; he coerced us—I know he did. In my case the police became peculiarly interested in my affairs about the same time that Glimmung first approached me. The way it worked out was that I more or less wound up having a choice between picking up on Glimmung's proposition or going to jail as a political prisoner."

In the name of god, Joe thought. Perhaps Glimmung played a hand in getting the QCA to drop in on me. And then the harness bulls who hung over me when I was giving away quarters, the cops who busted me—they may have been steered there by Glimmung!

Several people were talking at once, now. Listening intently, Joe made out the general drift of their discourses; they, too, were telling about rescues from police vehicles and stations by Glimmung. This changes everything, Joe said to himself.

"He got me to do an illegal act," a matronly woman was saying. "He got me to write a check to one of the government's beneficial organizations in a fit of passion. The check bounced and of course the police pulled me right in. When I got on this ship I jumped bail. I'm amazed they let me go, the QCA, I mean; I thought they'd stop me at the spaceport."

That is strange, Joe reflected. The QCA could have stopped all of us; Glimmung didn't take us to Plowman's Planet by some vast display of his power: he had us take a regular flight—was himself, in fact, at the spaceport, apparently to see that we didn't back out. Does that mean, Joe asked himself, that there is no genuine antagonism between Glimmung and the QCA?

He tried to remember the current law dealing with knowledge and skills of unusual value. It was a felony, he recalled, for a person to leave Earth if that person had skills which couldn't be made available to the government or "people" in his absence. My statement as to my skills and knowledge was routinely okayed, he remembered; they just glanced at it and stamped it and went on to the next one . . . and the next one was probably someone else, with a special and highly useful skill, on his way to Plowman's Planet. And they okayed him, too, it would seem.

He felt a deep and abiding insecurity, thinking this. A common basis between Glimmung and the police—if that were the case he was, for all intents and purposes, as much in the hands of the authorities as he would have been if he had remained at the police station. Perhaps even more so; on Plowman's Planet he would not be covered by the modicum of statutes protecting the accused. As someone had said already, once they reached Plowman's Planet they would be entirely in Glimmung's possession, for whatever he wanted done. They would be, in essence, extensions of Glimmung; it was another corporate existence toward which he was heading, and he had in no sense escaped from anyone or anything. And this would be true for all the others; hundreds or perhaps even thousands of them, flowing to Plowman's Planet from all over the galaxy. Jesus, he thought in despair. But then he thought of something, something that Glimmung, in humanoid form, had said in the restaurant of the spaceport. "There are no small lives." And the little fisherman of the night, as Glimmung had called the lowly spider.

"Listen," Joe said aloud into his microphone, and he had all the buttons down; everyone in the compartment was hearing him, whether they wanted to or not. "Glimmung told me something," he said, "at the spaceport. He told me about life waiting for something to come along and sustain it, and that thing, that event, never coming for many lives. He said that this Undertaking, this Raising of Heldscalla, was that thing, that event, for me." In his mind he felt his conviction grow until it became absolute and powerful, and he felt it change him; it woke him up until, by now, he could say, as Glimmung put it, *I am*. " 'Everything that has been latent,' Glimmung said, 'that has potential—all of it will be actualized.' I felt—" Joe hesitated, trying to find the exact word he wanted. "He knew," he said finally, as the other passengers listened in silence. "About my life. He knew it from the inside, as if he were inside it with me, looking out."

"He's telepathic," the timid little fellow piped up. There was a general stir of agreement.

"It was more than that," Joe said. "Hell, the police have equipment that manufactures telepathy and they use it all the time. They used it on me yesterday."

Miss Yojez said, "I experienced that also." To the others she said, "Mr. Fernwright is correct. Glimmung looked into the *basis* of my life; it was as if he saw all the way back through my life, saw it all pass along and lead here, to this point. And he saw that at this point it isn't worth living. Except for this."

"But he conspired with the police—" the gray-haired man said, but Miss Yojez interrupted him.

"We don't know that he did. I think we're experiencing panic. *I think Glimmung planned this Undertaking to save us.* I think he saw us all, the futilities of our various lives, and where they were leading, and he loved us, because we were alive. And he did what he could to help us. The Raising of Heldscalla is only a pretext; all of us—and there may be thousands—are the real purpose of this." She paused a moment and then said, "Three days ago I tried to kill myself. I attached the tube of my vacuum cleaner to the tailpipe of my surface car, and then I put the other end of the tube inside the car and I got in and started the motor."

"And then you changed your mind?" a slender girl with wispy, cornsilk hair asked.

"No," Miss Yojez said. "The turbine misfired and knocked

the tube loose. I sat for an hour in the cold for nothing."

Joe said, "Would you have tried again?"

"I planned to do it today," she said levelly. "And this time in a fashion that wouldn't fail."

The red-faced red-haired man said, "Hear what I have to say, for what it's worth." He sighed, a ragged, hoarse noise of resignation and unease. "I was going to do it, too."

"Not me," the gray-haired man said; he looked exceedingly angry; Joe felt the strength of the man's wrath. "I signed on because there was a great deal of money involved. Do you know what I am?" He glanced around at all of them. "I'm a psychokineticist, the best psychokineticist on Earth." Grimly he reached out his arm and a briefcase at the rear of the compartment flew directly toward him. Fiercely, he grabbed it, squeezing it.

—Squeezing it, Joe thought, the way Glimmung squeezed me.

"Glimmung is here," Joe said. "Among us." To the gray-haired man he said, "You are Glimmung and yet you're violently arguing against our trusting him. You."

The gray-haired man smiled. "No, friend. I'm not Glimmung. I'm Harper Baldwin, psychokineticist consultant for the government. As of yesterday, anyhow."

"But Glimmung is here somewhere," a plump woman with tangled doll-hair said; she was knitting and had said nothing up until now. "He's right, that man there."

"Mr. Fernwright," the stewardess offered helpfully. "May I introduce you to one another? This attractive girl beside Mr. Fernwright is Miss Mali Yojez. And this gentleman . . ." She droned on, but Joe did not listen; names weren't important, except, perhaps, the name of the girl seated beside him. He had, during the last forty minutes, become more and more favorably inclined toward her spare, sparse, even bleak beauty. Nothing at all like Kate, he thought to himself. The opposite. This is a truly feminine woman; Kate's a frustrated man. And that's the kind which castrates right and left.

Harper Baldwin, the introductions over, said in his overbearing, ultrafirm voice, "I think our status, our true status, is that of slaves. Let's stop a minute and review this whole matter, how we happen to be here. The stick and the carrot. Am I right?" He glanced from side to side, seeking confirmation.

"Plowman's Planet," Miss Yojez spoke out, "is not a backward, deprived planet. It has an advanced society active and evolving on it; true, it's not yet a civilization in the strict sense of the word, but it's not herds of food-gatherers nor even clans of food-planters. It has cities. Laws. A variety of arts ranging from the dance to a modified form of 4-D chess."

"That's not true," Joe said, with scathing anger. Everyone turned toward him, startled by his tone. "One vast old creature lives there. Apparently infirm. Nothing about an advanced city society."

"Wait a minute," Harper Baldwin said. "If there's one thing Glimmung is not it's infirm. Where'd you get your information, Fernwright? From the government encyclopedia?"

Joe said uncomfortably, "Yes." And secondhand, too.

"If the encyclopedia described Glimmung as infirm," Miss Yojez said evenly, "I'd be interested to know what else it said. I'm just curious to see how far your knowledge of Plowman's Planet departs from the reality situation."

With growing discomfort, Joe said, "Dormant. Advanced age; hence senile. Hence harmless." And harmlessness had not been apparent in Glimmung, at least as he had appeared to Joe. And to the others.

Standing, Mali Yojez said, "If you'll please excuse me—I think I'll go sit in the lounge and perhaps read a magazine or nap." In brisk, short steps she departed from the passenger compartment.

"I think," the plump woman busily knitting said, without looking up from her work, "that Mr. Fernwright ought to go to the lounge and apologize to Miss Whateverhernameis."

His ears red, and the back of his neck prickling, Joe got to his feet and followed after Mali Yojez.

As he descended the three carpeted steps an eerie feeling came over him. As if, he thought, I'm going to my death. Or is it life, for the first time? The process of being born?

Someday he would know. But not now.

6

He found Miss Yojez, as she had declared, seated in one of the great soft couches of the lounge, reading *Ramparts*. She did not look up at him, but he took it for granted that she was aware of him. Therefore he said, "How—do you happen to know so much about Plowman's Planet, Miss Yojez? I mean, you didn't get your knowledge out of the encyclopedia. Obviously. As I did."

Reading on, she said nothing.

After a pause Joe seated himself near her, hesitated, then, wondering what to say. Why had her statements about the society on Plowman's Planet angered him so? He didn't know; it seemed as irrational to him now as it had seemed to the others. "We have a new game," he said, finally. She continued reading. "You search the archives for the funniest headlines ever printed, each player topping the others." She still did not speak. "I'll tell you the headline that struck me as the funniest," he said. "It was hard to find; I had to look all the way back to 1962."

Mali glanced up. Her face showed no great emotion, no resentment. Merely detached curiosity, of a social nature.

No more. "And what was your headline, Mr. Fernwright?"

"ELMO PLASKETT SINKS GIANTS," Joe said.

"Who was Elmo Plaskett?"

"That's the point," Joe said. "He came up from the minors; nobody ever heard of him. That's what makes it funny. I mean, Elmo Plaskett—he came up for one day, hit one home run—"

"Basketball?" Miss Yojez asked.

"Baseball."

"Oh yes. The game of inches."

Joe said, "You have been on Plowman's Planet?"

For a moment she did not answer and then she said, simply, "Yes." He noticed that she had rolled the magazine into a tight cylinder, holding it with both hands, very tightly. And her face showed severe stress.

"So you know firsthand what it's like. And you encountered Glimmung?"

"Not really. We knew he was there, half-dead or half-alive; whichever way you'd put it . . . I don't know. Excuse me." She turned away.

Joe started to say something further. And then he saw, in a corner of the lounge, what appeared to be an SSA machine. Getting to his feet he went over to it and inspected it.

"May I be of help, sir?" a stewardess said, and approached him. "Would you like me to seal the lounge off so that you and Miss Yojez can make love?"

"No," he said. "I'm interested in this." He touched the control panel of the SSA machine. "How much does it cost to use it?"

"SSA service is free during your flight for one time," the stewardess said. "After that it takes two genuine dimes. Do you want me to set it up for you and Miss Yojez?"

"I'm uninterested," Mali Yojez spoke up.

"How unfair to Mr. Fernwright," the stewardess said, still smiling, but, in her voice, conveying a reprimand. "He can't use it alone, you understand."

"What do you stand to lose?" Joe asked Mali Yojez.

"You and I has no future together," she answered.

"But that's the whole point of the SSA machine," Joe protested. "To find out what—"

"I know what it finds out," Mali Yojez interrupted. "I've used they before. Okay," she said abruptly. "So you can see how it works. As a—" She searched for the word. "Experience."

"Thanks," Joe said.

The stewardess began setting up the SSA machine in a rapid, efficient fashion, meanwhile explaining it. "SSA stands for *sub specie aeternitatis;* that is, something seen outside of time. Now, many individuals imagine that an SSA machine can see into the future, that it is precognitive. This is not true. The mechanism, basically a computer, is attached via electrodes to both your brains and it swiftly stores up immense quantities of data about each of you. It then synthesizes these data and, on a probability basis, extrapolates as to what would most likely become of you both if you were, for example, joined in marriage, or perhaps living together. I will have to shave two spots of hair on both your heads, please, in order to attach the electrodes." She brought out a little stainless steel instrument. "How far ahead are you interested in?" she asked as she shaved the two spots on Joe's skull and then on Mali Yojez's. "A year? Ten years? You're free to choose, but the less time-elapse you pick, the more accurate the extrapolation will be."

"A year," Joe said. Ten years seemed too remote; probably he would not even be alive, then.

"Is that agreeable to you, Miss Yojez?" the stewardess asked.

"Yes."

"It will take the computer fifteen to seventeen minutes to gather, store, and process all the data," the stewardess said, as she attached two electrodes to Joe's scalp and then two to Mali Yojez's. "Merely sit still and relax; there is of course no discomfort; you won't feel a thing."

Mali Yojez said tartly, "You and I, Mr. Fernwright. Together a whole year. What a mellow, friendly year."

"You did this before?" Joe asked. "With another man?"

"Yes, Mr. Fernwright."

"And the extrapolation was unfavorable?"

She nodded.

"I'm sorry I rubbed you the wrong way, back there," Joe said, feeling humble and profusely apologetic.

"You called me a—" Mali Yojez flipped through her dictionary. "A liar. In front of all. And I have been there and you have not."

"What I meant to say—" he began, but the stewardess interrupted him.

"The SSA computer is gathering data from your minds, now. It would be best if you would relax and not quarrel for a time. If you could sort of gently free-float . . . let your minds open, open wide and let the probes gather data. Think of nothing in particular."

That's hard to do, Joe reflected. Under these circumstances. Maybe, he thought, Kate was right about me; in ten minutes I managed to insult Miss Yojez, my flight companion and an attractive girl. . . . He felt gloomy and oppressed. All I have to offer her is ELMO PLASKETT SINKS GIANTS. But maybe, he thought suddenly, she would be interested in pot-healing. Why didn't I talk about that the first time around? he asked himself. After all, that's the basis on which we're here: our skills, experience, knowledge, training.

"I'm a pot-healer," he said aloud.

"I know," Mali Yojez said. "I read your biographical material; remember?" But she did not sound so miffed, now. Her hostility, conjured up by his ineptness, had abated.

"Are you interested in pot-healing?" Joe asked.

"I'm fascinated by it," she answered. "That's why I so—" She gestured, then again consulted her dictionary. "Delighted. To sit and talk with you. Tell me—is the pots perfect again? Not mended but . . . like you say; healed."

Joe said, "A healed ceramic piece is in the exact condition as before it broke. Everything fuses; everything flows. Of course, I have to have all the pieces; I can't do it with a fraction of the pot not present." I'm beginning to talk like she does, he said to himself. She must be a strong personality and I'm subconsciously sensing this. As Jung pointed out, there is the anima archetype, which men experience when they encounter women. The archetypal image projected onto first one woman and then the next, giving them a charismatic power. I had better be careful, he reflected. After all, my involvement with Kate suggests that my anima-figure is strong-willed and dominating, rather than receptive and passive. I don't want to make the same mistake all over again, he said to himself. The mistake called Katherine Hurley Blaine.

"The SSA computer has obtained the data," the stewardess informed him and Mali Yojez. She removed the electrodes from their scalps. "It will take two or three minutes for it to process them."

"What form does its extrapolation take?" Joe asked. "Written on a paper ribbon in punch form, or—"

"You will be presented pictorially with a representative moment of your two lives entwined together a year from now," the stewardess said. "Projected in 3-D and color on the far wall." She lowered the lights in the lounge.

"Can I smoke?" Mali Yojez said. "We're not bound by Terran law out here."

"The smoking of tobacco cigarettes is forbidden on the ship during its entire flight," the stewardess said. "Because of the high oxygen content of the retained atmosphere."

The lights dimmed; everything around Joe sank into cloudy darkness, and each object became indistinct, including the girl beside him. A moment passed, and then an illuminated square materialized, in depth, near the SSA machine. Colors flashed by; colors and variegated images: he saw himself at work healing pots; he saw himself eating dinner; he saw her seated at her vanity table combing her hair. The images continued to flutter past, and then, all at once, the visual representation locked into place.

He saw, in 3-D and in color, himself and Mali holding hands and walking, slowly, along the twilight beach of some deserted, other world. The fish-eye lens-system zoomed in, and he saw his own face and hers. Both their faces expressed the most tender love possible. He knew at once, seeing his expression a year from now, that he had never had such a look on his face; life had never held anything like that before for him. Perhaps, he thought, it had never held this for her either. He glanced toward her but could not make out her features; he could not see how she was taking this.

"My, but you two look happy," the stewardess said.

Mali Yojez said, "Please leave us. Now."

"Well," the stewardess said. "I'm very sorry I was here at all." She left the lounge; the door clicked after her.

"They're everywhere," Mali Yojez said, by way of explanation. "The entire flight. They never leave you. Leave alone."

"But she showed us how the mechanism worked," Joe said.

"Hell, I can make a SSA machine work; I've it several times done." She sounded cross and tense, as if what she saw did not appeal to her.

"It looks like we'd be good for each other," Joe offered.

"Oh Christ!" Mali Yojez screeched; she banged her fist down on the arm of her chair. "That's what it said before. I and Ralf. Perfect outworking in everywhere. And it were not!" Her voice sank to a husky growl; her anger pervaded the lounge, as palpable as animal musk. He felt her glowering next to him; he intuited her immense emotional reaction to the representative scene projected by the machine.

"As the stewardess explained," Joe said, "the SSA mechanism can't see the future; it can only put together all the data from my mind and yours and work out a trend of greatest probability."

"Why then use it at all?" Mali Yojez countered.

"Consider it like fire insurance," Joe said. "You're sort of putting yourself in the position of claiming fraud because your rooming house didn't burn down after all, in other words that you really didn't need the insurance."

"The analogy is imperfect."

Joe said, "Sorry." He, too, felt irritable, now. And, as before, at her.

"Do you think," Mali said bitingly, "that I'm to go to bed with you because of this scene of us holding our hands? Tunuma mokimo hilo, kei dei bifo ditikar sewat," she said in her own tongue; obviously profanity.

There sounded a knock on the door. "Hey, you two," Harper Baldwin bawled. "We're working out the logistics of our collective employment; we need both of you."

Joe got up and made his way through the darkness of the lounge to the door.

For two hours they haggled. And at no time did they reach any kind of joint conclusion.

"We just don't know enough about Glimmung," Harper Baldwin complained, looking weary. He then scrutinized Mali Yojez intently. "I have the feeling that you know more about Glimmung than any of us, and a lot more than you'll admit. Hell, you even kept back from us the fact that you ever were on Plowman's Planet; if you hadn't mentioned it to Fernwright—"

"Nobody asked her," Joe said. "Until I did. And she said so, straight out."

A muffled, gangly youth asked, "What do you think, Miss Yojez? Is Glimmung trying to help us, or has he in effect created a slave population of experts for his own ends? Because if it's the latter we better get this ship turned around before we get any closer to Plowman's Planet." His voice squeaked with nervousness.

Seated beside Joe, Mali Yojez leaned toward him and said in a low voice, "Let's get out of here; let's go back to the lounge. We are getting nowhere and I want to talk to you farther."

"Okay," he said, pleased; he stood up and so did she. Together they made their way down the aisle toward the lounge.

"There they go," Harper Baldwin complained. "What's the great attraction about the lounge, Miss Yojez?"

Mali paused and said, "We besport ourself amorously." She then continued on.

"You shouldn't have told them that," Joe said as he and she entered the lounge and closed the door. "They probably believed you."

"But it's true," Mali said. "A person doesn't normally use the SSA machine unless he's serious. To the other person, in this case I." She seated herself on the couch of the lounge and reached up her arms toward him.

He locked the lounge door first. It seemed, all circumstances considered, a reasonable thing to do.

Joys too fierce, he thought, too fierce to be expressed. Whoever said that understood.

7

In orbit around Plowman's Planet, the ship began firing its retrorockets, cutting its velocity. They would be landing in half an hour.

Meanwhile, Joe Fernwright amused himself in a mordant way: by reading *The Wall Street Journal;* he had found over the years that this newspaper, out of all of them, contained the most chilling and the most recent oddities. Reading the *Journal* was like taking a little trip into the future—six months or so.

A new deep-depth rooming house in New Jersey, designed especially for geriatric persons, has built into it a novel circuit, designed to make the transfer of the room easy and without delay. When a roomer dies, electronic detectors in the wall register his lack of pulse, and send swift circuits into action. The deceased is grappled by standard waldoes, drawn into the wall of the room, where on the spot his remains are incinerated within an asbestos chamber, thus permitting the new tenant, also a geriatric case, to take possession by noon.

He ceased reading, tossed down the newspaper. We must be better off out here, he decided. If that's what they've got planned for us back on Earth.

"I've verified our reservations," Mali said matter-of-factly. "We all have rooms at the Olympia Hotel in the largest city on the planet; Diamond Head, it's called, because it's on a winding prominence that goes fifty milies out into Mare Nostrum."

"What's 'Mare Nostrum'?" Joe asked.

" 'Our Ocean.' "

He showed the item in the *Journal* to her and then, silently, to the rest of the passengers. They all read it and then they all looked at one another for sign of a reaction.

"We made the right choice," Harper Baldwin said. The others nodded. "That's good enough for me," Baldwin said. He shook his head and scowled, disgust and anger contorting his face. "And we built such a society," he rasped.

Strong-armed members of the ship's crew manually unscrewed the hatch; outside air eddied in, smelling odd and cold. It seemed to Joe that the ocean was close; he sensed it in the air. Shielding his eyes he gazed out against a weak sun; he distinguished the outline of a reasonably modern-looking city, and, past it, hills in a mixture of brown and gray. But the ocean is somewhere nearby, he said to himself. Mali is right; this is a planet dominated by an ocean. And it is in the ocean that we will find everything that matters.

Smiling with mechanical courtesy, the stewardesses escorted them to the open hatch and the flight of stairs which led down to the damp surface of the field. Joe Fernwright took Mali by the arm and led her down; neither of them spoke for a time—Mali seemed absorbed in herself, taking no notice of the other people or the spaceport buildings. Bad memories, Joe reflected. Maybe what happened to her happened here.

And for me, he thought; look what this is for me. The first interplanetary or intersystem flight in my life. This ground under me is not Earth. A very strange and important thing is happening to me. He smelled the air. Another world and another atmosphere. It feels strange, he decided.

"Don't say," Mali said, "that you find this place 'unearthly.' Please, for my sake."

"I don't get it," Joe said. "It is unearthly. It's completely different."

"Never mind," Mali said. "A little game Ralf and I had. A long time ago. Thingisms, we called them. Let's see if I can remember some of them. He thought all of them up. 'The book business is hidebound.' That's one. 'Plants are taking over the world sporadically.' Let's see. 'The operator let me off the hook.' I always liked that; it made me think of a giant hook, in fact a whole giant phone. 'In 1945 the discovery of atomic energy electrified the world.' Do you see?" She glanced at him. "You don't," she said. "Never mind."

"They're all true statements," Joe said. "As far as I can make out. What's the game part?"

" 'The senate inquiry into modern use of side arms was muzzled.' How do you like that one? I saw that in a newspaper. I think Ralf found the others in newspapers or heard them over TV; I think all they were real." She added somberly, "Everything about Ralf was real. For the beginning. But then later, no."

A careful, brown, large creature resembling a rat approached Joe and Mali. It held what appeared to be an armload of books.

"Spiddles," Mali said, pointing to the careful ratlike creature, and to a second one which had accosted Harper Baldwin. "One of the native life-forms, here. Unlike Glimmung. You will find—let me see." She counted on her fingers. "Spiddles, wubs, werjes, klakes, trobes, and printers. Left over from the old days . . . all of them older species, when the Fog-Things of antiquity passed away. It wants you to buy a book."

The spiddle touched a tiny tape recorder mounted on its belt; the tape began to speak for the spiddle. "Fully documented history of a fascinating world," it said in English, and then evidently repeated this in a variety of other tongues; anyhow it had stopped speaking in English.

"Buy it," Mali said.

"Pardon?" Joe said.

"Buy its book."

"You know this book? What book is it?"

Mali said, with rigorous patience, "There is only one book. In this world."

"By 'world,' " Joe said, "you mean 'planet,' or in the larger sense—"

"On Plowman's Planet," Mali said, "there is just this one book."

"Don't the people get tired of reading it?"

"It changes," Mali said. She handed the spiddle a dime, which it accepted gratefully; a copy of the book was passed to her and she in turn passed it to Joe.

Examining it, Joe said, "It has no title. And no author."

"It is written," Mali said, as they walked on toward the spaceport buildings, "by a group of creatures or entities—I don't the English know—that records everything that passes on Plowman's Planet. Everything. Great and small."

"Then it's a newspaper."

Mali halted; she turned to face him, her eyes burning with exasperation. *"It is recorded first,"* she said, as steadily as she could manage. "The Kalends spin the story; they enter it in the ever-changing book without a title, and it comes to about, finally."

"Precognitive," Joe said.

"That raises a question. Which is cause? Which is effect? The Kalends wove in their altering, evolving script that the Fog-Things would pass away. They did pass away. Did then the Kalends *make* them pass away? The spiddles think so."

She added, "But the spiddles are very superstitious. They naturally believe that."

Joe opened the book at random. The text was not in English; he did not recognize the language or even the letters of its alphabet. But then, as he leafed through it, he came to a short section in English, embedded in the mass of alien-looking entries.

> The girl Mali Yojez is an expert at removing coral deposits from submerged artifacts. Other individuals brought from various systems throughout the galaxy include geologists, structural engineers, hydraulic engineers, seismologists; one specializes in underwater robot operations and another, an archaeologist, is a master at locating buried, ancient cities. A peculiar many-armed bivalve lives in a tank of salt water and functions well in supervising the raising of sunken ships for salvage purposes. A gastropod, capable of

At that point the text lapsed into another language; he shut the book, pondered. "Maybe I'm mentioned in here somewhere," he said, as they reached the moving sidewalk leading to the concourse sections of the spaceport terminal building-complex.

"Of course," Mali said calmly. "If you long look enough you will find it. How will you make it—pardon. How will *it* make *you* feel?"

"Eerie," he said, still pondering.

A surface car, acting as a taxi, transported them to their hotel. Joe Fernwright, on the short trip, continued to examine the untitled book; it preoccupied him, preempting the colorful shops which the taxi passed, and the several life-forms bustling about here and there—he was aware of the city street, its people, and buildings, but only dimly. Because he had already found another passage in English.

Obviously, the Undertaking involves the locating of and the raising and repair of an underwater structure, probably—due to the number of engineers involved—of great magnitude. Almost certainly an entire city or even an entire civilization, very likely of some remote past age.

And then, once again, the text lapsed into a foreign script resembling dots and dashes, a sort of binary system of annotation.

Joe said to the girl beside him in the taxi, "The people who are writing this book know about the raising of Heldscalla."

"Yes," Mali said shortly.

"But where's the precognition?" Joe demanded. "This is remarkably up to date—right up to this minute, give or take an hour—but that's all."

"You will find it," Mali said, "when you have looked a long time. It is buried. Among the different texts, which are all translations of one primary text, one line like a thread. The thread of the past entering the present, then entering the future. Somewhere in that book, Mr. Fernwright, the future of Heldscalla is written. The future of Glimmung. The future of us. We are all woven in by the yarn of the Kalends' time, their time-outside-of-time."

Joe said, "And you already knew about this book, before the spiddle sold it to you."

"I saw it before when Ralf and I were here. The SSA machine extrapolated we'd be joyous, and the Kalends' book, this book, said Ralf would—" She paused. "He killed himself. First he tried to kill me. But—he wasn't able to."

"And the Kalends' book said that."

"Yes. Exactly that. I remember it, Ralf and I reading in the text about ourselves and not believing. Still under the idea that the SSA mechanism was scientific data-analysis and this book was tale by old wife, a lot of old wives, seeing doom when we and the SSA machine saw happihood."

"Why did the SSA machine miss?"

"It missed because it didn't have one datum. Whitney's Syndrome. Psychotic reaction to amphetamines by Ralf. Paranoia and murderous hostility. He thought himself overweight; he took them as—" She hunted for the word.

"Appetite suppressants," Joe said. "Like alcohol." Good for some people, he thought; lethal for others. And Whitney's Syndrome didn't require overdoses; even a small amount triggered it off. If the latent illness was already there. Just as, for an alcoholic, the smallest drink meant defeat and bitter, utter, final destruction. "Too bad," he murmured.

The taxi pulled up to the curb. Its driver, a beaverlike creature with wicked, cutting teeth, said several words in a language which Joe did not understand; Mali, however, nodded and gave the beaverish individual a sum of metal money from her purse, and then she and Joe stepped from the taxi onto the sidewalk.

Joe, looking around him, said, "It's like going back a hundred and fifty years." Surface cars, carbon arc lighting . . . this could be Earth in the days of President Franklin Roosevelt, he thought to himself, both enticed and amused. He liked it. The pace, he realized; it's slower. And the density of population—relatively few organisms propelled themselves up and down the street, either on foot (or a reasonable substitute) or in cars.

"You can see why I got angry at you," Mali said, catching his reaction. "For your defaming Plowman's Planet, my home for six years. And now—" She gestured. "I'm back. And doing again what I did then: believing faith in a SSA mechanism."

"Let's go inside the hotel," Joe said, "and have a drink."

Together, they passed through the revolving door, into the Olympia Hotel, with its wooden floors, carved hardwood decorations, polished brass doorknobs and railings, and thick red carpet. And its antique elevator, which Joe had already caught sight of. Nonautomatic, he discovered. The elevator required an attendant.

In his hotel room, with its dresser, splotched mirror, iron bed, and canvas windowshade elegance, Joe Fernwright sat on an overstuffed, faded chair and studied The Book.

Not long ago he had been preoccupied with The Game. And now—The Book. But this consisted of something quite different, and the more he read of The Book the more he realized it. Gradually, as he nosed among its pages, he began to assemble, in his mind, the totality of the English text; he had begun to put the separate bits in superimposition over one another.

"I'm going to take a bath," Mali said. She had already opened her suitcase and had laid most of her clothes out on the bed in her room. "Isn't it strange, Joe Fernwright?" she called. "That we have to keep two rooms. Like a century ago."

"Yes," he said.

She entered the room, wearing only her tight pants; bare from the waist up, he saw. Small-breasted but dense and tall, with fine muscle tone. The body of a dancer, he said to himself, or—a Cro-Magnon female, a hunter, an astute, supple person accustomed to long, lean, even fruitless marches. There was not a gram of useless flesh on her, as he had already discovered in the locked lounge of the ship. He had clutched it then; now he saw it. However, he thought morbidly, Kate had—actually still has—as good a figure. That made him depressed. He returned to reading The Book.

"Would you have wanted to go to sleep with me," Mali said, "if I were a cyclops?" She pointed to a spot above her nose. "One eye there. Polyphemus; the cyclops in *The Odyssey*. They put his one eye out with a burning stick, I think."

Joe said, "Listen to this." He read aloud from The Book. " 'The current, dominant species on the planet consists of what is called a Glimmung. This shadowy, enormous entity is not native to the planet; it migrated here several centuries ago, taking over from the weak species left over when the once-ruling master species, the so-called Fog-Things of antiquity, vanished.' " Joe waved her to come and look. " 'Glimmung's power, however, is sharply curtailed by a mysterious book in which, it is alleged, everything which has been, is, and will be is recorded.' " He snapped the book shut. "It's talking about itself."

Coming over to his chair, Mali bent to read the text. "Let me see what else it says," she said.

"That's all. The English part ended there."

Taking The Book from him, Mali began to glance through it. She had begun to frown; her face was tense and stern. "Well here you are, Joe," she said at last. "As I told. You're in here by name."

He took The Book from her and read rapidly.

Joseph Fernwright learns that Glimmung considers the Kalends and their Book his antagonist, and is said to be plotting to undermine the Kalends once and for all. How he will do this, though, is not known. Here the rumors begin to differ.

"Let me turn the pages," Mali said; she examined the subsequent pages and then, her face darkening, paused. "In my language," she said. For a long, long time she studied the passage, and as she read and reread it, her expression became more intense, shadowed by her own intense urgency into starkness. "It says," she said at last, "that Glimmung's Undertaking is the raising of the cathedral Heldscalla to dry land once more. *And that he will fail.*"

"Is there more?" Joe said. He had a feeling there was; her face showed it.

Mali said, "It says that most of those recruited to help Glimmung will be destroyed. When the Undertaking fails." She corrected herself. "Tóojic. Damaged or made to unexist.

Maimed; that's it. They will be permanently altered, beyond immediate repair."

"Do you think Glimmung knows about these passages?" Joe said. "That he'll fail and we'll be—"

"Of course he knows. It's there in the text, in that section you read. 'Glimmung considers the Kalends and their book his antagonist and plots to undermine them.' And, 'He's raising Heldscalla to undermine them.' "

"It didn't say that," Joe said. "It reads, 'How he will do this, though, is not known; here the rumors begin to differ.' "

"But obviously it's the raising of Heldscalla." She paced about the room in agitation, her hands clasped tightly together. "You said it yourself. 'The people who are writing this book know about the raising of Heldscalla.' All you have to do is put the two passages together. I told you it was all there, our future, Heldscalla's, Glimmung's. And ours is to unexist, to die." She halted, stared at him frantically. "That's the way the Fog-Things perished. They challenged the Book of the Kalends. As the spiddles can tell you; the spiddles are still chattering about it."

Joe said, "We had better tell the rest of the people here at the hotel about it."

A knock sounded on the door; it opened, and Harper Baldwin peered apologetically into the room. "I'm sorry to bother the two of you," he rumbled, "but we've been reading this book." He held up his copy of the Book of the Kalends. "There's stuff in it about all of us. I'm having the hotel management notify all its guests to meet in the main conference room in half an hour."

"We'll be there," Joe said, and, beside him, Mali Yojez nodded, her partially disclosed body rigid with concern.

8

Half an hour later all of them, a hotelful of sentient organisms of forty kinds, filled the main conference room. Joe, looking about at the enormous variety of life-forms, saw, among them, several which he had eaten, back on Earth. Most of the forms he did not recognize. Glimmung had in fact gone to many star-systems to get the talent he wanted. More than Joe had realized.

"I think," Joe said quietly to Mali, "that we ought to prepare ourselves for a full manifestation of Glimmung. He'll probably show up here as he really is."

Mali grated, "He weighs forty thousand tons. If he manifested himself here as he really is he'd collapse the building; he'd fall through the floor and down to the basement."

"Then in some other form. Such as that of a bird."

On the stage, at the microphone, Harper Baldwin rapped for silence. "Come on, folks," he said, and, in all that vast variety of tongues needed, his words were translated into each earphone.

"You mean such as a chicken?" Mali said.

Joe said, "That's not a bird; a chicken is fowl, barnyard fowl. I mean like a soaring great long-winged albatross."

"Glimmung isn't above lowly things," Mali said. "Once he manifested himself to me—" She broke off. "Never mind."

"What this meeting is about, folks," Harper Baldwin continued, "has to do with a book they have here that we've run across; now, those of you who've been on this planet longer probably know about it. If so, you've already formed your own—"

A multilegged gastropod rose up and spoke into its microphone. "Of course we are familiar with The Book. The spiddles sell it at the spaceport."

Mali said into her own mike, "Our edition, being later than yours, may contain material you haven't read."

"We buy a new edition each day," the gastropod said.

"Then you know it says that—the raising of Heldscalla will fail," Joe said. "And that we'll be killed."

"It does not precisely say that," the gastropod answered. "It says that those he employs will *suffer,* will receive some sort of blow which will permanently change them."

An immense dragonfly took the floor by the simple expedient of flying up to Harper Baldwin's entrenchment and landing on his shoulder. Challenging the gastropod it said, "There is no doubt, however, that the Book of the Kalends predicts the failure of the attempt to raise Heldscalla."

The gastropod yielded the floor to a reddish jelly supported by a metal frame that held it upright; hence it could join in the discussion. As it spoke it flushed darkly, obviously very shy. "The burden of the text seems to state that the raising of the cathedral will fail. 'Seems to state,' I put it to you. I am a linguist, brought here by Mr. Glimmung for that reason; under the water in the cathedral there are countless documents. The key sentence, 'The Undertaking will fail,' appears one hundred and twenty-three times in The Book. I have read each of the translations and I submit that the text most properly means, 'There will be failure after the Undertaking,' that it will *lead* to failure, rather than *it* will fail."

"I don't see the difference," Harper Baldwin said, frowning. "Anyhow the part that's important for us is the part about our being killed or injured—not the failure of the Undertaking. Isn't this Book always right? The creature that sold it to me said it was."

The reddish jelly said, "The creature who sold that Book gets forty percent of the purchase price for itself. Naturally it says The Book is accurate."

Stung by the jibe, Joe hopped to his feet. "Then by the same token you could indict all the doctors in the universe on the grounds that they make money when you're sick, so they're responsible for your being sick when you're sick."

Laughing, Mali tugged him back down into his seat. "Oh god," she said, covering her mouth. "I don't think anyone's defended the spiddles in two hundred years. Now they have a—let's see. A champagne."

"Champion," Joe growled, still feeling the heat of resentment. "It's our lives," he said to her, "that we're talking about. This isn't a political debate or a taxpayers' meeting about the local transportation."

An undercurrent of muttering moved about the room. The craftsmen and scientists were talking among themselves.

"I move," Harper Baldwin brayed, "that we act collectively, that we form a permanent organization with officers who can deal as a deputation with Glimmung for the rights of us all. But before that, all of you friends and coworkers seated here today, or flying around the room here today, I suggest that we take an initial vote as to whether we want to work on the Undertaking at all. Maybe we don't want to. Maybe we want to go home. Maybe we ought to go home. Let's see how we feel collectively about it. Now, how many vote to go ahead and work—" He broke off. A vast rumbling shook the conference room; Harper Baldwin's voice had become inaudible. Talk, for any of them, was now out of the question.

Glimmung had come.

It must be the true manifestation, Joe decided as he watched and listened. It was in all respects the real Glimmung, Glimmung as he actually was. And so—

Like the sound of ten thousand junked, rusty automobiles being stirred by one giant wooden spoon, Glimmung heaved himself up and onto the raised stage at the far end of the conference room. His body quivered and shuddered, and from deep inside him a moan became audible. The moan grew, rose, until it became a shriek. An animal, Joe thought. Caught, perhaps in a trap. One paw. And it's trying to get loose but the trap is too complicated. And, at the same time, a great spewing forth of brackish sea water, trash fish, aquatic mammals, sea kelp—the room reeked with the roar and shock of the sea. And, in the center of all of it, the churning lump which was Glimmung.

"The hotel people aren't going to like this," Joe said half aloud. Good god—the huge mass of fluttering extremities, the whipping, writhing arms which flung themselves at every spot on the gigantic carcass . . . the whole thing heaved, and then, with a furious roar, it collapsed the floor beneath it; the mass disappeared from sight, leaving remnants of the sea all over the room. From the gaping chasm smokelike tendrils, probably steam, fizzled upward. But Glimmung was gone. As Mali had predicted, his weight had been too great. Glimmung was down in the basement of the hotel, ten floors below them.

Shaken, Harper Baldwin said into his microphone, "A-a-apparently we'll have to go downstairs to talk to him." Several life-forms hurried over to him; he listened, then straightened up and said, "I understand he's in the cellar rather than on the next floor. He—" Baldwin gestured in agitation. "—evidently went the whole way down."

"I knew it would happen," Mali said. "If he tried to come here. Well, we'll have to conduct our words with him in the cellar." She and Joe both got to their feet; they joined the crowd of life-forms gathered at the elevators.

Joe said, "He should have come as an albatross."

9

When they reached the basement, Glimmung boomed a hearty greeting at them. "You won't need translating equipment," he informed them. "I'll speak to each of you telepathically in your own language."

He filled almost all of the basement; they had to remain by the elevators. Now he had become more dense, more compact—but he still remained huge.

Joe took a large, deep, steadying breath and said, "Are you going to pay the hotel compensation? For the damage you've done?"

"My check," Glimmung said, "will be in the mail by tomorrow morning."

"Mr. Fernwright just meant that as a joke," Harper Baldwin said nervously. "About paying the hotel."

" 'Joke'?" Joe said. "Collapsing ten floors of a twelve-floor building? How do you know people weren't killed? There could be as many as a hundred dead, plus a lot more injured."

"No, no," Glimmung assured him. "I killed no one. But the query is legitimate, Mr. Fernwright." Joe felt the presence of Glimmung within him, stirring in his brain: Glimmung edged here and there throughout the most unusual corners of Joe's mind. I wonder what he's looking for? Joe thought. And at once the answer, within his consciousness, came. "I'm interested in your reaction to the Book of the Kalends," Glimmung said. He spoke, then, to them all. "Out of all of you, only Miss Yojez knew about The Book. The rest of you I'll need to study. It will only take a moment." The extension of Glimmung left Joe's mind, then. It had gone elsewhere.

Turning to Joe, Mali said, "I'm going to ask him a question." She, too, took a deep and steadying breath. "Glimmung," she said sharply, "tell me one thing. *Are you going to die soon?*"

The enormous lump throbbed; its whiplike extremities thrashed in agitation. "Does it say that in the Book of the Kalends?" Glimmung demanded. "It does not. If I were, it would say."

Mali said, "Then The Book is infallible."

"You have no reason to think I am near death," Glimmung said.

"None at all," Mali said. "I asked my question in order to learn something. I learned it."

"When I am depressed," Glimmung said, "I begin to think about the Book of the Kalends, and I think that their prediction that I cannot raise Heldscalla is true. That, in fact, I can accomplish nothing; the cathedral will remain at the bottom of Mare Nostrum into eternity."

Joe said, "But that's when your energy is low."

"Each living entity," Glimmung said, "passes through periods of expansion and periods of contraction. The rhythm of living is as active in me as in any of you. I am larger; I am older; I can do many things that none of you, even collectively, can. But there are times when the sun is low in the sky, toward evening, before true night. Small lights come on, here and there, but they are a long way off from me. Where I dwell there are no lights. I could of course manufacture

life, light, and activity around me, but they would be extensions of myself alone. This, of course, is changed, now that
you have begun to come here. The group today is the final
group; Miss Mali Yojez and Mr. Fernwright and Mr. Baldwin,
and those with them, are the last who will be coming."

I wonder, Joe thought, if we will leave this planet again.
He thought about Earth and his life there; he thought about
The Game and his room with its dead, black window; he
thought about the government's Mickey Mouse money that
came in baskets. He thought of Kate. I won't be calling her
again, he thought. For some reason I know that; it is a fact.
Probably because of Mali. Or perhaps, he thought, the larger
situation . . . Glimmung and the Undertaking.

And Glimmung's falling through the floor, he thought.
Descending ten stories and winding up in the basement. That
meant something, he realized, and then he realized something else. Glimmung knew his weight. As Mali had said, no
floor could hold him. Glimmung had done it on purpose.

So we wouldn't be afraid of him, Joe realized. When we
at last saw him as he really is. Then, he thought, we really
should be afraid of him, perhaps. More so than before. Just
exactly because of this.

"Afraid of me?" Glimmung's thought came.

"Of the whole Undertaking," Joe said. "There's too little
chance of it being a success."

"You are right," Glimmung said. "We are talking about
chances, about possibilities. Statistical probabilities. It may
work; it may not. I don't claim to *know;* I am only hoping.
I have no certitude about the future—*nor does anyone else,
including the Kalends.* That is the basis of my entire position.
And my intent."

Joe said, "But to try and then to fail—"

"Is that so terrible?" Glimmung said. "I'll now tell you all
something about yourselves, something that every one of you
possesses: a quality in common. You have met failure so often
that you have all become afraid to fail."

I thought so, Joe thought. Well, so it goes.

"What I am doing," Glimmung said, "is this. I am attempting to learn how much strength I have. There is no abstract way of determining the limits of one's force, one's ability to exert effort; it can only be measured in a way such as this, a task which brings into view the actual, real limitation to my admittedly finite—but great—strength. Failure will tell me as much about myself as will success. Do you see that? No, none of you can. You are paralyzed. That's why I brought you here. Self-knowledge; that is what I will achieve. And so will you: each about himself."

"Suppose we fail?" Mali asked.

"The self-knowledge will be there anyhow," Glimmung said; he sounded baffled, as if there was a gap between himself and the group of them. "You really do not understand, do you?" he said to them all. "You will, before it's over. Those of you, anyhow, who want to go through with it."

A fungiform lispingly asked, "At this late point do we still have the right to choose?"

"Any of you who wish to return to your own world are free to do so," Glimmung said. "I will provide passage— first class—back. But those of you who do go back—you will find it once again as it was. And, as it was, you could not live such a life; each of you intended to destroy yourselves, and were in the process of so doing when I found you. Remember. That is what lies behind you. *Don't make it that which lies ahead of you.*"

There was an uncomfortable silence.

"I'm leaving," Harper Baldwin said.

Several others moved closer to him, signifying that they would leave, too.

"What about you?" Mali asked Joe.

Joe said, "What's behind me is the police." And death, he thought. The same as for you . . . for us all. "No," he said. "I'm going to try. I'll take the chance that he—we— fail. Maybe he's right; maybe even failure is valuable. As he says, it tells us the limit of ourselves; it maps our boundaries."

"If you'll give me a tobacco cigarette," Mali said, with a shiver of fear, "I'll stay, too. But I'm dying for a cigarette."

"That's nothing worth dying for," Joe said. "Let's die for this. Even if we fall ten stories into the basement doing it."

"And the rest of you are staying," Glimmung said.

"That's right," a univalvular cephalopod squeaked.

Uneasily, Harper Baldwin said, "I'll stay. I guess."

Glimmung, with satisfaction, said, "Then let us begin."

At the curb before the Olympia Hotel heavy-duty trucks had been parked. Each had a driver and each driver knew what to do.

A portly organism with a long, ropy tail approached Joe and Mali, a clipboard clutched energetically in its fuzzy paw. "You two are to go with me," the organism declared, and then picked from the group eleven more individuals.

"That's a werj," Mali said to Joe. "Our driver. They can make excellent speed; their reflexes are so acute. We'll be out on the promontory in the manner of a minute."

"Matter of minutes," Joe corrected absently as he seated himself on the bench in the rear segment of the truck.

Other life-forms squeezed in with Joe and Mali, and then the truck engine came noisily to life.

"What kind of turbine is that?" Joe said, annoyed by the noise it made.

A kindly looking bivalve beside him groaned, "It's internal combustion. Bang bang bang all the way."

"The frontier," Joe said, and felt an aching joy, all at once. Yes, he thought, this is the frontier; we are back with Abraham Lincoln in a log cabin, and Daniel Boone, all of them. The oldtime pioneers.

One by one the trucks pulled away from the curb, their lights yellow in the night, like the orbs of luminous, foreign moths.

"Glimmung will be waiting for us," Mali said. "When we

get there." She sounded tired. "He's capable of reflex relocation, based on autonomic pulsations emanating from within his own neurological substructure. For all intents and purposes he can move from one locus to another without time-lapse." She rubbed her eyes and sighed.

The helpful bivalve spoke up once more. "The creature beside you, Mr. Fernwright, is truthful." It extended a pseudopodium to Mali. "Miss Yojez, I am Nurb K'ohl Dáq from Sirius three. We have all been waiting anxiously for your party to arrive, because we understood that once you reached the Hotel Olympia all of us who have been waiting a long time can begin. As it seems to be so. But in addition I am glad to become known to you and have you know me, in that I for my part will search out and locate the coral encrusted objects which will then be brought out of Mare Nostrum and brought to you at your shop."

"I am the engineer in charge of discreet artifacts and the transporting thereof on Mr. Nurb K'ohl Dáq's request to your shop," a quasiarachnid, brightly black in its chitinous exoskeleton, said.

"You haven't done any preliminary work?" Mali asked it. "While you waited?"

"Glimmung kept us in our rooms," the bivalve explained. "We did two things. One. We read all pertinent documents relating to the history of Heldscalla. Two. We watched on a video monitor as robot sensors scanned the sunken cathedral time and again. On our screens we have seen Heldscalla countless times. But now we will be allowed to touch it."

"I wish I could go to sleep," Mali said. She rested her close-cropped head on Joe's shoulder and slumped against him. "Wake me up when we get there."

The quasiarachnid said to Joe and the bivalve, "This total Undertaking . . . it reminds me of an Earth saga, parts of which we were required to memorize during our educational years. It made a deep impression on me."

"He means the Faust theme," the bivalve told Joe. "Faus-

tian man, striving upward, never satisfied. Glimmung is like
Faust in certain respects, unlike him in others."

Rustling its antennae in agitation the quasiarachnid said,
"Glimmung resembles Faust in all respects. The Faust, at
least, of Goethe, which is the version I adhere to."

Eerie, Joe thought. A chitinous multilegged quasiarachnid
and a large bivalve with pseudopodia arguing about Goethe's
Faust. A book which I've never read—and it originated on
my planet, is the product of a human being.

"Part of the difficulty," the quasiarachnid was saying, "lies
in the translation; it was written in a language which has died
out."

"German," Joe said. He knew that much, at least.

"I have," the quasiarachnid muttered, "made a—" It
groped in a plastic utility pouch slung over its shoulder; four
of its manual extremities busily sorted through the pouch.
"Damn thing," it muttered. "Everything sinks to the bottom.
Here it is." It brought out a much-folded sheet of paper,
which it proceeded to unfold carefully. "I have made my own
translation into modern-day Terran, formerly called 'English.' I will read you the crucial scene from the second part,
the moment at last when Faust pauses in contemplation of
what he has done, and is content. May, can—whatever the
expression is. All right, Mr. Fernwright, sir?"

"Sure," Joe said, as the truck rumbled along, over potholes
and rocks, shaking and swaying the creatures within it. Mali,
now, seemed to have totally fallen asleep. She had certainly
been right about the driving skill of the werj; the truck rattled
through the darkness at a great rate.

" 'A swamp surrounds the mountains,' " the quasiarachnid
read from its carefully preserved sheet of paper. " 'Poisoning
everything already reclaimed. To drain the foul marsh—this
must be done; this would be the highest conquest possible.
I'll open room for many millions: not in any sense safe, but
daily freed, in which to live. Green the meadow, and fruitful;
men and herds almost already on the most new earth, settled

on the rim of which has been pushed up by bold peoples'
efforts. Within here a paradise land, that keeps outside the
flood, and as it eats away, trying to enter and take over, a
group will hurries to cut it off. Yes! This—' "

The bivalve interrupted the quasiarachnid's earnest reci-
tation. "Your translation is not idiomatic. 'Men and herds
almost already on the most new earth.' Grammatically it is
correct, but no Terran talks like that." The bivalve waved a
pseudopodium toward Joe, seeking his support. "Isn't that
so, Mr. Fernwright?"

Joe thought, "Men and herds almost already on the most
new earth." The bivalve was right, of course; but—

"I like it," Joe said.

Highly pleased, the quasiarachnid yelped, "And see how
much it resembles us and Glimmung, the Undertaking!
'Within here a paradise land, that keeps outside the flood.'
The flood is a symbol for everything that eats away structures
which living creatures have erected. The water which has
covered Heldscalla; the flood won out many centuries ago,
but now Glimmung is going to push it back. 'A group will'
which hurries to cut it off—that is all of us. Perhaps Goethe
was a precog; perhaps he foresaw the raising of Heldscalla."

The truck slowed. "We're there," the werj driver informed
them. He applied his brakes, and the truck came to a squeak-
ing halt, causing everyone aboard to pitch violently. Mali
stirred, opened her eyes; she glanced around in each direction, panic shaping her face—obviously she could not orient
herself immediately.

"We're there," Joe said to her, and hugged her against
him. And now it begins, he reflected. For better or worse.
For richer; for poorer. Until—death, he thought. Do us part.
Odd that he should think of that, the litany of the marriage
vows. Yet it seemed to fit. Death, in some indistinct form,
seemed to hover close by.

Stiffly, he rose, helped Mali up; they and the others began
creakily to get down from the back of the truck. The night

air with its smell of the sea . . . he took a deep breath. It is really close now, he realized. The sea. The cathedral. And Glimmung trying to separate them, the sea pushed back from Heldscalla. Like God did, he thought. Separating the dark from the light, or however it goes. And the water from the land.

To the quasiarachnid he said, "God, in Genesis, was very Faustian."

Mali moaned. "Good lord; theology in the middle of the night." In the damp, cold air she shivered, peering around her. "I don't see a damn thing. We're in the center of no-place."

Against the dim nocturnal sky Joe made out what appeared to be a geodesic dome. There it is, he said to himself.

The other trucks had arrived by now; all had stopped and from each of them the throng of life-forms emerged, each in its own peculiar fashion. Some helped others; the reddish jelly, for example, had a difficult time until a spiny apparition resembling a hostile bowling ball helped it down.

A hovercraft, illuminated and large, manifested itself above them, gradually descending until at last it had parked itself in the midst of their group. "Hello," it said. "I am your conveyance to your work-areas. Board me carefully and I will take you there, if you would, please. Hello, hello."

Hello to you, too, Joe said to himself as he and the rest of them slithered, flapped, and bumbled aboard.

Inside the geodesic dome they were met by a herd of robots. Joe stared in disbelief. Robots!

"They're not illegal here," Mali pointed out. "You must get it into your mind: you're not on Earth anymore."

Joe said, "But Edgar Mahan proved that a synthetic life-form can't come into existence. 'Life has to come from life, and therefore, in the construction of self-programming mech-anisms—' "

"Well, you're looking at twenty of them," Mali said.

"Why were we told they couldn't be made?" Joe asked her.

"Because there're too many unemployed people on Earth as it is. The government faked scientific evidence and documentation to say robots couldn't be done. They are rare, however. They are hard to build and costly. I'm surprised to see this many. It is all he has, I'm sure. This is a—" She searched for the word. "For our benefit. A display. To impress us."

One of the robots, catching sight of Joe, coasted directly toward him. "Mr. Fernwright?"

"Yes," Joe said. He looked around him at the corridors and massive doors and the recessed overhead lighting. Efficient, extensive, and labyrinthine. And without defect. Obviously it had just been built—and not yet put to use.

"I'm amazingly glad to see you," the robot declared. "In the center of my chest you will probably see the word 'Willis' stenciled. I am programmed to respond to any instruction beginning with that word. For example, if you would like to see your work-area, merely say, 'Willis, I would like to be taken to my work-area,' and I would then happily lead you there, giving pleasure to myself and hopefully to you as well."

"Willis," Joe said, "are there living quarters here for us? For example is there a private room for Miss Yojez? She's tired; she should be asleep."

"A three-room apartment is ready for you and Miss Yojez," Willis said. "Your personal living quarters."

"What?" Joe said.

"A three-room apartment—"

"You mean we have an actual *apartment*? Not just a room?"

"A three-room apartment," Willis repeated, with robotic patience.

"Take us there," Joe said.

"No," Willis said, "you have to say, 'Willis, take us there.' "

"Willis, take us there."

"Yes, Mr. Fernwright." The robot led them across the foyer to the elevators.

After looking over the apartment Joe got Mali into bed; she fell asleep without a sound. Even the bed was large. Everything in the apartment was solid and in good taste (of a modest sort), and the apartment itself was, like its contents, large. He could hardly believe it. He examined the kitchen, the living room—

And found, in the living room, on a coffee table, a jar from Heldscalla. As soon as he saw it he knew what it was. Seating himself on the couch he reached out and carefully picked it up.

The deep yellow glaze. He had never seen such a rich yellow before; it surpassed even the yellows of Delft tiles—surpassed, in fact, Royal Albert yellow. That made him wonder about bone china. Are there bone beds here? he asked himself. And, if so, what percentage bone are they using? Sixty percent? Forty? And are their bone beds as good as the peoples' bone bed in Moravia?

"Willis," he said.

"Yassuh."

Questioningly, Joe said, " 'Yassuh'? Why not 'Yessir'?"

The robot said, "I jes' done bin readin' Earth history, Massah Fernwright, suh."

"Are there bone beds here on Plowman's Planet?"

"Well, Massuh Fernwright, I don' rightly know. Ah gues' dat you'all kin as' de central computator iffen—"

"I order you to talk correctly," Joe said.

"You'all gotta say 'Willis' fust. Iffen you'all wan' me tuh—"

"Willis, talk correctly."

"Yes, Mr. Fernwright."

"Willis, can you take me to my work-area?"

"Yes, Mr. Fernwright."

"Okay," Joe said. "Take me there."

The robot unlocked the heavy steel and asbestos door and stood to one side, permitting Joe Fernwright to enter the enormous, dark room. Overhead lights came on automatically as he crossed the threshold.

He saw, at the far end of the room, a major workbench, and fully equipped. Three sets of waldoes. Glare-free lighting which operated from a pedal console. Self-focusing magnifying glasses, fifteen inches and more in diameter. The separate heat-needles, all the known sizes. To the left of the workbench he saw protective cartons, a kind which he had read about but never seen. Going over, he picked up one, dropped it experimentally . . . and watched it float downward, gently landing, without impact.

And the sealed containers of glazes. Every tint, shade, and hue was represented; the row of containers lined one side of the room in four rows. With them he could match virtually the glazes of every pot coming onto his bench. One more item. He walked over to it and inspected it with wonder. A weightless area, where gravity was balanced by a ring of invisible counterspin: this was the ultimate workshop device for a pot-healer, this weightless area. He would not need to secure the pieces of pot in order to meld them together; the pieces, in the weightless chamber, would simply remain where he put them. By means of this he could handle four times the number of pots he had turned out in former times, and those were times of prosperity. And the positioning would be absolutely exact. Nothing would slip, slide, or tilt during the healing process.

He noted, too, the kiln, which might be needed if a shard were missing and the need to create a duplicate came into being. Thus he could complete pots of which he did not have all the pieces. This aspect of the craft of pot-healing was not generally dealt with publicly, but—it existed.

Never in his life had he seen such a well-equipped shop for pot-healing.

Already, a number of broken pots had been brought in; a pile of filled protective cartons had accumulated at the incoming end of the bench. I could start right now, he realized. All I have to do is to flip a half-dozen switches and I'm in business. Tempting . . . He walked over to the rack of heat-needles, took one down, held it. Well balanced, he decided. Quality product; the best. He opened one of the filled cartons, gazed down at the potsherds. His interest became emergent instantly; setting down the heat-needle he took the shards out one by one, enjoying the glazes and the glaze texture of the pot. A fat, short pot. A funny pot, perhaps. He put the pieces back in the carton and turned, with the idea of carrying them over to the weightless area. He wanted to begin. This was his life. Never did I think, he thought, that I would have access to, the use of—

He halted. And felt, inside, as if some animal had gnawed at his heart. Gnawed it with greed. And delight.

A black figure, like a negative of life itself, stood facing him. It had been watching him, and now that he faced it he thought it would go away. But it remained. He waited a little longer. It still remained.

"What is this thing?" he asked the robot, who still stood at the threshold of the workroom.

"You have to say 'Willis' first," the robot reminded him. "You have to say, 'Willis, what—' "

"Willis," he said, "what is it?"

"A Kalend," the robot said.

10

With them, Joe Fernwright thought, there is not life but merely a synopsis of life. We are a thread that passes through their hands; always in motion, always flowing, we slip by and are never fully grasped. The slipping away is continuous, and carries all of us with it, on and on, toward the dreadful alchemy of the tomb.

To Willis he said, "Can you contact Glimmung?"

"You have to say—"

"Willis," he said, "can you contact Glimmung?" Across the room from him the Kalend stood silently—not silently as an owl might stand, absorbing and subduing noise with its feathers, but silent in the mechanical sense: as if its audio portion had been severed. Is it really there? Joe wondered. It appeared to be substantial; it did not have a ghostly, vaporous, wraithlike quality. It really is there, he said to himself. It has invaded my work-area before I have placed a single shard into the weightless chamber. Before I have ignited one heat-needle.

"I can't contact Glimmung," Willis said. "He's sleeping; this is his time for that. In another twelve hours he'll wake

up and then I can contact him. But he's left a large number
of servo-assist mechanisms ready, in case of an emergency.
Do you want any of them activated?"

Joe said, "Tell me what to do. Willis, tell me what the hell
to do."

"About the Kalend? There is no existing record of anyone
doing anything about Kalends. Do you want me to research
this further? There is one particular computer which I can
tie into; perhaps it can make an analysis of your abilities in
relation to the nature of the Kalend, and formulate a new
interaction which—"

"Do they die?" Joe said.

The robot remained silent.

"Willis," he said, "can they be killed?"

"That's hard to say," the robot said. "They're not your
standard living creature. Also, they all look alike, which
makes the problem even more complicated."

The Kalend laid a copy of The Book on the table beside
Joe Fernwright. And waited for him to pick it up.

Silently he picked up the book, held it for a time, and then
opened it to the page marked. The text read:

That which Joe Fernwright finds in the sunken cathedral
will cause him to kill Glimmung, and, in doing so, halt
forever the raising of Heldscalla.

That which I will find in the cathedral, Joe said to himself.
Down there, under the water. Already down beneath the
sea. Waiting for me . . .

He thought, I had better get under the water as soon as I
can. Will Glimmung let me? he wondered. Especially after
he has read this—and he is probably reading it right now,
as I stand here; certainly he follows every alteration of the
text as it grows, changes, corrects itself day after day. Hour
by hour.

If he is smart, Joe thought, he will kill me first. Before I go under water. Kill me, in fact, *now*.

He stood there, waiting for Glimmung's violence to come onto him.

It did not come. That's right, he remembered. Glimmung is asleep.

On the other hand, he meditated, maybe I should not go down there. What would Glimmung recommend? Perhaps that should decide it; if Glimmung wanted him to go under water and inspect the sunken cathedral then he would . . . if not, then not. Odd, he thought, that my first reaction would be to want to go under water. As if I can't wait to make my discovery—a discovery which will destroy Glimmung and with him the project of raising the cathedral. A perverse response, he decided. A slip on the part of unconscious inhibitions. Maybe this told him something about himself, something which he had not known. Something evoked by the Kalend and its Book. The Kalends woke this in me, he realized; this is the principle on which they operate. By this, they make their prophecy come true.

"Willis," he said, "how does one get down to Heldscalla?"

"One descends via suit and mask or via a prolepsis chamber," the robot said.

"Can you take me there?" Joe asked. "I mean, Willis—"

"Just a moment," the robot said. "There's a call coming through to you. An official call." The robot was silent for a moment. Then it said, "Miss Hilda Reiss, Glimmung's personal secretary. She wants to talk to you." A door in the robot's chest popped open and, out on a tray, came an audio telephone. "Pick up the receiver," Willis said.

Joe picked up the receiver.

"Mr. Fernwright?" a practiced, competent, female voice said, "I have an urgent request for you from Mr. Glimmung, who is now sleeping. He would prefer it if you did *not* go down to the cathedral right now. He wants you to wait until someone can go with you."

"You say 'request,' " Joe said. "Am I to assume that that's actually an order? That he's ordering me not to go below water?"

"All Mr. Glimmung's instructions," Miss Reiss said, "come in the form of requests. He does not order; he always merely requests."

"So this is, actually, an order," Joe said.

Miss Reiss said, "I think you understand, Mr. Fernwright. Sometime tomorrow, Mr. Glimmung will contact you. Goodby." The phone clicked, became dead.

"It's an order," Joe said.

"That's right," Willis the robot agreed. "That's the way he handles everything, as she cleverly pointed out."

"But if I tried to go below water—"

"Well, you can't," the robot said flatly.

"I can," Joe said. "I can do it and get fired."

"You can do it," the robot said, "and become killed."

" 'Killed,' Willis? Killed how and who by?" He felt frightened and angry, a peculiar mixture of emotions that started his vagus nerve into spasms; his breathing, his peristalsis, and his heart rate—all changed radically. "Killed by who?" he demanded.

"You first have to say—aw, the hell with it," the robot said. "Yes, many feral life-forms. Many hazards."

"But normal for a task of this kind," Joe said.

"I suppose you could say that. But a request like this—"

"I'm going under water," Joe said.

"You will find terrible decay down there. Decay which you cannot imagine. The underwater world in which Heldscalla lies is a place of dead things, a place where everything rots and falls into despair and ruin. *That is why Glimmung intends to raise the cathedral*. He is unable to endure it down there; neither will you be able to. Wait until he goes under water with you. Wait a few days; heal the pots in your workshop and forget about going below. Glimmung calls it the 'Aquatic

Sub-World.' He is right; it's a world made up of its own self, entirely separate from ours. With its own wretched laws, under which everything must decline into rubbish. A world dominated by the force of unyielding entropy and nothing else. Where even those with enormous strength, such as Glimmung, become vitiated and lose their power in the end. It is an oceanic grave, and it will kill all of us unless the cathedral can be raised."

"It can't be all that bad," Joe said, but, as he spoke, he felt fear rustle through him and lodge inside his heart, fear generated in part by the vacuity of his own remark.

The robot looked at him enigmatically, a complex look that gradually became that of scorn.

"Considering you're a robot," Joe said, "I don't see what you have emotionally involved in this; you have no life."

The robot said, "No structure, even an artificial one, enjoys the process of entropy. It is the ultimate fate of everything, and everything resists it."

Joe said, "And Glimmung expects to halt this process? If it's the ultimate fate of everything, then Glimmung can't halt it; he's doomed. He'll fail and the process will go on."

"Down below the water," Willis said, "the decay process is the only force at work. But up here—the cathedral raised—there will be other forces which do not move in a retrograde manner. Forces of sanction and repair. Of building and making and form-creating—and, in your case, healing. That is why you are so needed. It is you and the others like you who will forestall the decay process by your abilities and work. Do you see?"

"I want to go down there," Joe said.

"Suit yourself. I mean that literally; put on diving gear and descend into Mare Nostrum, alone, in the night. Descend into the subworld of decay and see it for yourself. I'll take you to one of the staging centers floating on Mare Nostrum; you can descend from there—without me."

"Thanks," Joe said. He uttered the word with what he intended to be irony; however, it emerged in a weak wheeze, and the robot did not seem to catch his tone.

The staging center consisted of a platform within hermetically sealed domes, three of them, each large enough for life-forms to gather, with their equipment. Joe gazed about him in expert appreciation at the size of the construct. Built with robot labor, he decided. And recently; the domes seemed new, and probably were so. This installation had been created for him and the others, and would not be used until he and they began to operate out of them. Space, he reflected, is not at a premium, here, as it is on Earth. These domes can be as large as they want . . . and Glimmung, of course, had wanted them large indeed.

"And you still won't descend with me," he said to the robot Willis.

"Never."

"Show me the diving gear," Joe said. "And show me how to use it. Show me everything I need to know."

"I will show you the minimal—" the robot began, and then broke off. On the roof field of the greatest dome a small airship was landing. Willis scrutinized it intently. "Too small for Glimmung," he murmured. "It must be a more meager and hence lesser life-form."

The airship came to a stop; it remained immobile and then its hatch slid back. Taxi, it proclaimed from its stem to its stern. And out of the taxi stepped Mali Yojez.

She descended via the elevator and came directly toward Joe and the robot Willis. "Glimmung spoke to me," she said. "He told me what you're doing here. He wanted me to go along with you. There was some doubt in his mind as to whether you could make it alone—I mean physically survive the experience of the Sub-World down there."

"And he thinks you can," Joe said.

"He thinks that two of us going together and having each

other to rely on—he thinks that that would probably work. And I'm more experienced than you. Vastly more."

"Mrs. Lady," Willis said to her, "did Glimmung want me to go undersea, too?"

"He didn't mention you," Mali said tartly.

"It's just as well." The robot scowled in heavy gloom. "I dislike it down there."

"But soon," Mali said, "it will all be changed. There will *be* no 'down there.' Only up here, in this world, where other laws operate."

"The best-laid plans of mice and men," the robot said, with frigid skepticism.

"Help us into our gear," Joe said.

The robot said, "Down there in the Aquatic Sub-World, you will be in a place that Amalita has forgotten."

"Who is 'Amalita'?" Joe asked.

Mali said, "The god for whom the cathedral was built. The god who was worshiped in Heldscalla. When the cathedral is restored, then Glimmung can call upon Amalita, as in earlier times, before the Catastrophe in which the cathedral sank. The defeat of Amalita by Borel—a temporary defeat, but a major one. I am reminded of a Terran poem by Bert Brecht called, 'The Drowned Girl.' Let's see; if memory serves . . . 'And gradually God forgot her, first her arms, then her legs and body until she was—' "

Joe said, "What sort of deities are these?" There had been no mention of this before, but of course it was obvious and logical; a cathedral was a place in which to worship, and someone or something had to be the object of the worship. To Mali, he said, "Do you know anything more about this angle?"

"I can fully inform you," the robot said, annoyed.

To it, Mali said, "Had it ever occurred to you that it might be Amalita, working through Glimmung, who is raising the cathedral? So that worship of him here on this planet can resume?"

"Hmm," the robot said, in a nettled fashion; Joe could almost hear it whir and click as it cogitated. "Well," it said all at once, "anyhow you asked about the two deities, Mr. Sir. However, you once again neglected to say—"

"Willis," Joe said, "tell me about Amalita and Borel. How long have they been worshiped, and on how many planets? And where did the cult begin?"

"I have a brochure," the robot said, "which will exhaustively cover these matters." It slid its hand into its thorax pocket; from the pocket it lifted out a mimeographed pamphlet. "I wrote this in my spare time," the robot said. "With your permission I will refer to it. That way I don't have to overtax so much in my memory spools. To begin with, Amalita existed alone. That was roughly fifty thousand Terran years in the past. Then, in a spasm of apotheosis, Amalita felt sexual desire. But there was nothing to feel sexual desire toward. He felt love, and there was nothing to love. He felt hate, and there was nothing to hate."

"He felt apathy. And there was nothing to feel apathetic about." Mali spoke without emotion; it did not involve her.

"Let's tackle sexual desire first," the robot said. "As is well known, the most enjoyable form of sexual love is that which pertains to incest, inasmuch as incest is the fundamental taboo throughout the universe. The greater the taboo, the more sheer excitement. Hence, Amalita created his sister, Borel. The next most exciting aspect of sexual love is love for someone evil, someone who, if you didn't love them, you would abominate them. So Amalita caused his sister to be evil; she began at once to tear down everything which he had, over the centuries, built."

Mali murmured, "Such as Heldscalla."

"Yes, Mrs. Lady," the robot agreed. "Now, the next most powerful stimulant to sexual love is to be in love with someone stronger than you. So Amalita caused his sister to be capable of destroying his edifices one by one; he tried to intervene, but she was by now too strong. As he had intended. Finally, the last element: the love object forces one to descend to its level, where its laws, unethical and violent, obtain. This is what we have here in the Raising of Heldscalla. Every one of you will have to descend into the Aquatic Sub-World in which Amalita's laws do not operate. Even Glimmung himself will inevitably sink into the Sub-World where Borel's travesty of reality cloaks everything and is everywhere."

"I thought of Glimmung as a deity," Joe said. "Because of his immense power."

The robot said, "Deities do not fall ten floors to the basement."

"That seems reasonable," Joe admitted.

"The criteria involved," the robot said, "start with immortality. Amalita and Borel have that; Glimmung has not. The second criterion deals with—"

"We are aware of the two other criteria," Mali interrupted. "Unlimited power and unlimited knowledge."

"Then you've read my pamphlet," the robot said.

"Christ," Mali said with withering disdain.

"You mention Christ," the robot said. "He is an interesting deity because he has only limited power; he has only partial knowledge; and he could die. He fulfills none of the criteria."

"Then how did Christianity come into being?" Joe said.

"It came into being," the robot said, "because this is what Christ did: he worried about other people. 'Worry' is the true translation of the Greek *agape* and the Latin *caritas*. Christ stands empty handed; he can save no one, not even himself. And yet, by his concern, his esteem, for others, he transcends—"

"Just give us the pamphlet," Mali said wearily. "We'll read it in our spare time. As of now, we're going under the water. Get our diving gear ready, as Mr. Fernwright asked."

"There is a somewhat similar deity," the robot said, "on Beta twelve. This deity learned how to die whenever another creature on his planet died. He could not die in place of them, but he could die *with* them. And then, as each new creature was born, he was restored. So he has endured countless deaths and rebirths. As compared with Christ, who died only once. This, too, is dealt with in my pamphlet. Everything is in my pamphlet."

"Then you're a Kalend," Joe said.

The robot eyed him. Long and carefully. And silently.

"And your pamphlet," Joe said, "is the Book of the Kalends."

"Not exactly," the robot said, at last.

"Meaning what?" Mali demanded sharply.

"Meaning that I have based my various pamphlets on the Book of the Kalends."

"Why?" Joe said.

The robot hesitated and then said, "I hope to be a freelance writer someday."

"Get our gear," Mali said, with overwhelming weariness.

An odd, random thought entered Joe's mind. Possibly it had emerged because of the discussion about Christ. " 'Worry,' " he said aloud, echoing the robot's term. "I think I know what you mean. A strange thing happened to me, once, back on Earth. A very small thing. I got down a cup from the cupboard, a cup I hardly ever used. In it I found a spider, a dead spider; it had died because there was nothing for it to eat. Obviously it had fallen into the cup and couldn't get out. But here's the point. It had woven a web, at the bottom of the cup. As good a web as it could weave under the circumstances. When I found it—saw it dead in the cup, with its meager, hopeless web—I thought, It never had a chance. No flies would ever have come along, even if it had waited forever. It waited until it died. It tried to make the best of the circumstances, but it was hopeless. I always wondered, Did it know it was hopeless? Did it weave the web knowing it was no use?"

"Little tragedy of life," the robot said. "Billions of them, unnoticed, every day. Except that God notices, at least according to my pamphlet."

"But I see what you mean," Joe said. "About worry. Concern; that's closer to it. I felt it concerned me. It *did* concern me. *Caritas*. Or in the Greek—" He could not remember the word.

"Can we go below, now?" Mali asked.

"Yes," Joe said. Obviously she did not understand. But, oddly, the robot did. Strange, Joe thought. Why does it understand when she doesn't? Maybe *caritas* is a factor of intelligence, he reflected. Maybe we've always been wrong: *caritas* is not a feeling but a high form of cerebral activity, an ability to perceive something in the environment—to notice and, as the robot had put it, to worry. Cognition, he realized; that's what it is. It isn't a case of feeling versus thinking: cognition is cognition.

Aloud he said, "Can I have a copy of your pamphlet?"

"Ten cents, please," the robot said, holding out the pamphlet.

Joe fished out a cardboard dime and handed it to the robot. To Mali he said, "Now let's go below."

11

The robot touched a switch; a wall locker opened its sliding door and Joe saw, within, complete sets of diving gear: oxygen masks, pedal flippers, plastic skinsuits, waterproof light sources, weights, pry bars, crossbows, oxygen and helium tanks—everything. Including many assorted items of equipment which he could not identify.

"In view of your lack of experience in deep-sea diving," the robot said, "I would suggest you descend by spherical prolepsis chamber. But, if you want to suit up—" It shrugged. "I have no control over that; the decision is yours."

"I've had sufficient experience," Mali said briskly. She began bringing equipment out of the locker; presently she had a formidable heap stacked neatly before her. "Get out what I got out," she instructed Joe. "Put the segments of the suit on in the order I'm putting them on, and in the same way."

They suited up and then, led by Willis, they made their way to the staging chamber proper.

"Some time," the robot said as it unscrewed the great plug-valve in the floor of the chamber, "I intend to write a pamphlet on deep-sea diving. There is a basic assumption that the chthonic world is in the ground—you find this in every religion. But in actuality it's in the ocean. The ocean—" It dragged the huge plug away. "—is the actual primordial world, out of which every living thing came a billion years ago. On your planet, Mr. Fernwright, this error is found in many religions—for instance, the Greek goddess Demeter and her daughter Kore—they come up from the earth."

Mali said to Joe, "There is attached to your belt an emergency device in case of failure in the oxygen circuit of your rig. If you lose your air, if the conduit loosens or bursts or the tanks run dry, activate the hypo plunger of the belt unit." She pointed to the one mounted on her own belt. "It swiftly drops metabolic processes so that your need for oxygen is minimal; little enough so that you can easily float to the surface before you suffer any brain damage or experience any other lasting physiological effect from the curtailed oxygen supply. When you float to the surface you will of course be unconscious, but your mask is designed to let in air automatically; it will respond to the altered condition, the presence of outside air. And then I'll be up to steer you back here."

" 'I must be gone,' " Joe quoted, trying to remember how it went. " 'There is a grave where daffodil and lily wave.' "

The robot said, " 'And I would please the hapless faun, buried under the sleepy ground.' A favorite of mine. Yeats, I believe. Do you think, Mr. Sir, that you are descending into a grave? That what stands before you is death? That to descend is to die? Answer in twenty-five words or less."

"I know what the Kalend told me," Joe said somberly. "What I find in Heldscalla will cause me to kill Glimmung. So it is into death that I'm going; maybe not *my* death, but someone else's. To permanently halt the raising of Heldscalla." Grimly, the words flowed within his mind, always at the surface. Always available. They would not sink out of sight for a long, long time. Perhaps, he thought, never. The stigma is upon me and I will carry it the rest of my life.

"I will give you a lucky charm," the robot said; again it rummaged within its chest pocket. It presently brought out a tiny packet, which it handed to Joe. "A token which represents the purity and sublimity of Amalita. A symbol, so to speak."

"And it'll ward off evil influences?" Joe asked.

The robot said, "You must say, 'Willis, will it ward—' "

"Willis," Joe said, "will this charm help us down there?"

After a pause the robot said, "No."

"Then why did you give it to him?" Mali asked caustically.

"To—" The robot hesitated. "Never mind." It seemed, then, to retract into itself; it became silent. Distantly inert.

"I'm going to lash us up in tandem," Mali said to Joe as she attached a cable from her belt to his. "This will give us twenty feet of free line. That should be enough. I can't risk getting separated from you; that might be the last we'd see of you."

The robot wordlessly handed Joe a plastic carton.

"What for?" Joe said.

"You probably will find a broken pot or two down there. And you'll want to bring the shards up."

Stalking catlike to the aperture in the floor of the staging chamber, Mali said, "Let's go." She snapped on her helium-powered torch, glanced briefly at Joe, and then dived out of sight. The twenty-foot cable attached to him stretched taut, pulled him; it walked him to the aperture, propelling him, and then, his mind blank of any real thoughts, he dived, too. Passively.

The light of the staging chamber faded out above him. He snapped on his own torch and allowed himself to be tugged along, down and down; the water became utterly black, except for the vague, seemingly half-real quadrant illuminated by his torch. And, below him, Mali's torch glowed, like the phosphorescent light of an exceedingly deep sea-fish.

"Are you okay?" Mali's voice sounded in his ear; it startled him and then he realized that a two-way intercom connected them.

"Yes," he said.

Various fish floated past him, incurious and pompous; they gawked at him and traveled on, disappearing into the void surrounding his illuminated path.

"That windbag robot," Mali said scathingly. "My god; we must have conversed with it for twenty minutes."

But, Joe thought, we are here, now. Within the waters of Mare Nostrum, spiraling down and down.

I wonder, he thought, how many theologically inclined robots there are in the universe. Perhaps Willis was the only one . . . put there by Glimmung to talk at extended length, thus interfering with the attempt to go below the surface.

The heat unit of his suit snapped on; he felt the cold of the sea ebb away from him. And for that he gave thanks.

"Joe Fernwright," Mali's voice sounded in his ear. "Did it occur to you that Glimmung might have sent me here, to go below with you as we're doing, *to kill you*? Glimmung knows the prophecy. Wouldn't it be reasonable for him to do that? So obvious. Didn't you think at all of that?"

As a matter of fact he had not. And, thinking it now, he felt the chill of the ocean ease back into its grip around him; the enervating cold plundered his loins, his heart—he felt himself freeze, within, into frightened immobility, like a defenseless minor creature; his fear deprived him of his sense of being human, and of being a man. It was not a man's fear; it was the fear of a small animal. It shrank him, as if devolving him into ages past; it eradicated the contemporary aspects of his self, his being. God, he thought. I am feeling a fear that is millions of years old.

"On the other hand," Mali pointed out, "the text which the Kalend showed you might have been a forgery, prepared for your benefit. One single copy for your eyes alone."

Joe said hoarsely, "How did you know about the Kalend and the new text?"

"Glimmung told me."

"Then he read what I read. It isn't a forgery for my benefit. If it was you wouldn't be here."

She laughed. And said nothing. And, on and on, they spiraled downward.

"Then I can assume I'm right," Joe said.

Stark and yellow, the hull of something gleamed and putrified within the focus of his torch. To his right, Mali's torch lit up another vertebra of it. Huge . . . like an ark that had been built to contain every living thing—and an ark which had sunk to the bottom of Mare Nostrum. Forever. The ark, he thought, of failure.

"What is it?" he asked Mali.

"A skeleton."

"Of what?" He thrashed toward it, sweeping out as much of it as possible with his torch. Simultaneously, Mali did the same.

She bobbed close to him, then; he could see her face through the transparent plastic disk of her oxygen mask. When she spoke, her tone was subdued, as if, despite her knowledge and experience, she had not expected to find this here.

"It's a Glimmung," she said. "The skeleton of an ancient, archaic, long-dead, forgotten Glimmung; it's coral-encrusted terribly; it's been down here, I would say, for a century at least. Good lord."

"You mean you didn't know it was here?" he demanded.

"Maybe Glimmung; not me. But—" She hesitated. "I think it's a Black Glimmung."

"What's this?" Joe asked, and his uneasiness burgeoned; it filled him and became, by degrees, overwhelming dread.

"It's almost impossible to explain," Mali said. "As with antimatter; you can talk about it but you can't really imagine what the words mean. There are Glimmungs and there are Black Glimmungs. Always on a one-to-one ratio. Each individual Glimmung has his counterpart, his opaque Doppelgänger. Sooner or later, during his life, he must kill his Black counterpart, or it will kill him."

"Why?" Joe said.

"Because that's the way it is. It's like asking, 'Why is a stone?' Do you see? They—*evolved* this way, on this strange parity basis. They are mutually exclusive, antagonistic entities, or, if you prefer, properties. Yes, properties, like chemical combinations. You see, the Black Glimmungs are not precisely alive. And yet they're not biochemically inert either. They're like malformed crystals with the form-destroying principle motivating them; tropic specifically as regards their matching Glimmung. And some say that it's not limited to Glimmungs; some say—" She broke off, staring acutely ahead. "No," she said. "Not this. Not already; not the first time."

A decaying hump of flopping fabric mingled with threads of cloth tottered toward them, propelled by the currents of murky water. It had a humanoid look, as if once, long ago, it had held itself erect, had walked on strong legs. Now it bowed from the waist, and its legs dangled as if the bones had been scooped out of them. He stared at it and it came nearer and he continued staring, because it seemed somehow to want to eddy into his vicinity . . . clumsily, so that its pace was slow. And yet it made progress forward. He made out its face, now.

And felt the world within him disintegrate.

"It's your corpse," Mali said. "You must understand; time down here is simply not—"

"It's blind," he said. "Its eyes—they've—rotted away. Gone. Can it see me?"

"It's aware of you. It wants—" She hesitated.

"What does it want?" he demanded, snarling at her so that she shuddered.

"It wants to talk to you," she said, then. And became totally silent; now she merely observed, merely saw. And did nothing, in either direction. She did not assist him; she did not assist his corrupted corpse. As if, he thought, she has withdrawn and is not here. I am alone with this *thing*.

"What should I do?" he asked her.

"Not—" She became silent once more, then abruptly said, "Don't hear what it says."

"You mean it can speak?" he demanded, appalled. He could accept what he saw; he could retain his sanity when presented with his own dead body. But he could not believe beyond that. It could not be real, not sane; it had to be the mimicry of some aquatic life-form, something which saw him and managed, in a plastic manner, to adopt the semblance of his own shape.

"It will tell you to go away," Mali said. "To leave this world, this ocean. Leave Heldscalla forever, and Glimmung's hopes, his project. See: it's already trying to form words."

The decayed flesh of the lower face writhed; he saw broken teeth and then, from within the cavity which his mouth had become, noise issued forth. A drumming, as if far off on a heavy ocean cable. Something extending for five hundred miles, something which weighed so much. Something so dense, so hard to maneuver. And yet the thing tried. The drumming continued. And finally, as it bobbed before him, rotating slow motion and rising now, then sinking a little, he distinguished one word. Then another.

"Stay," it said, and its mouth cavity gaped. Small fish floated in, disappeared, then floated skimmingly back out. "You—must go ahead. Ahead. Lift. Heldscalla."

"Are you still alive?" he asked it.

Mali said, "Nothing down here is really alive, in the strict sense. Residual amounts . . . partial changes in a damaged battery."

"But it's not yet," he said. "This is the future."

"There is no future down here," Mali said.

"But it hasn't happened to me yet. I'm alive. I'm facing this ugly thing, this horrible mobile rot. It couldn't talk to me if I were it."

"Obviously," Mali said. "But—the distinction isn't really complete between the two of you. Some of it is merged in you; some of you remains in it. They are both you; you are both of them. 'The child is father to the man'; remember? And the man is father to the corpse. But I thought it would say to you to go away. And instead he—it—wants you to remain. That's what it's swum up here to tell you. I don't understand. This can't be your Black, in the sense that I was explaining it, anyhow. It's badly decayed but it's benign, and the Blacks are never benign. Can I ask it something?"

He said nothing. Mali took it as silent assent.

"How did you die?" she asked the corpse.

The exposed jawbone waggled whitely in the currents of water surrounding it as it drummed out its deformed words, its answer. "Glimmung had us killed."

" 'Us'?" she asked alertly. "How many of us? All of us?"

"Us." It extended a decomposed arm toward Joe. "We two." It became silent, then. And, by degrees, drifted away. "But it isn't so bad. I have a box I've made; it helps protect me. I get inside it and put up a barrier where the door—the entrance—is, and very few of the fish, the really dangerous fish, get in."

"You mean you're trying to protect your *life*?" Joe said. "But your life is over." He did not comprehend; it made no sense, and it was eerie and bizarre. The thought of a decayed corpse—his corpse—living this semilife down here, going though the motions of making itself safe . . . "Improve living standards for the dead," he said savagely, speaking at large, to neither Mali nor the corrupted body floating before him.

"The curse," Mali said.

"What?" he said.

"It won't let you go. It confronts you with your own final self and yet you won't go away. And then later on when you're this—" She gestured at the corpse. "You'll wish you had left. Today, tonight. Tomorrow morning."

"Stay," the corpse said to Joe.

"Why?" he said.

"When Heldscalla is raised from the water I will go to sleep. I am waiting to go to sleep; I'm glad you came, at last. I have waited centuries. Until you come here and release me I am caught in the totality of time." It made an imploring gesture with its right arm and hand, but portions of the hand broke loose and fell away into the murky water; the hand now had only two fingers, and, seeing this, Joe felt physically, substantially, sickened. He thought, If I could turn the clock back and not have come here. But the corpse had said the opposite; his coming here meant its—and his—release. My good Jesus, he thought. I'll be that thing before long; parts of my body will fall off and be snapped up by the dangerous fish. I will have to hide in a box down here at the bottom of the sea, and the fish will eat me piece by piece.

Or maybe it's not true, he thought. Maybe this is not my corpse; how many people are confronted by their own corpse—a corpse talking beseechingly? The Kalends, he thought. But that made no sense because—contrary to Mali's expectations—it had urged him to stay, urged him to begin his job of pot-healing.

Glimmung, he thought. This is a phantasm projected by him, a warped, a deranged hook, to gaff me. Obviously.

He said to the bobbing, lingering corpse, "Well, thanks for your advice. I'll take it under advisement."

"Is my corpse here, too?" Mali demanded.

No answer. Joe's physical remnants had floated away. Did I say the wrong thing? Joe asked himself. But ye gods; what are you supposed to say to your own corpse? I said I'd think its advice over; what more can it ask? He felt strangely angry, not frightened any longer or horrified, just the mundane boiling inside him of irritability. Pressure like this—it was unfair. He had been told that he *must* go ahead with his part of the project. And then he thought of the curse.

"Death," he said to Mali as they bobbed close to each other. "Death and sin are connected. That means that if the cathedral is cursed then we also—"

"I'm going back up." She rose, drifting upward above him, her legs moving expertly. "I don't want to find myself too close to the dredging operation." She pointed.

He turned his body in that direction.

An enormous, silent instrument, a construct which he did not recognize, lay far to their right. He heard its activity now, the dull, low throbbing. Its sound had been there all this time; but, he estimated, in the form of a twenty cycles per second churning at the lower limit of audibility. Perhaps he had felt it as a vibration; perhaps he still felt it that way now. "What is it?" he asked her, and started in that direction; it fascinated him.

"A caprix scoop," Mali said. "Ionian caprix, the element with the greatest atomic weight currently in use. Replacing the older rexeroid scoops that you used to see."

"Is the entire cathedral going to be raised by the scoop?" he asked Mali, who, unwillingly, flapped and dove beside him, following his course in a reluctant, halting manner.

"Only the base," Mali said.

"The rest is being cut into blocks?"

"Everything but the base, which is a solid slab of Deneb three agate. If it were sawed into blocks it would be unable to support the superstructure. Hence the scoop." She hung back. "It's not safe to go so close. Anyhow you've seen caprix scoops and shovels in operation before; you know the principle they utilize. The fulcrum is passed back and forth among the four rims of the scoop. Now please! Let's go back up to the surface. I find it very exacting down here. Damn it; it's dangerous so near the dredging."

"Are all the blocks cut?" he asked.

"Oh god," Mali said wearily. "No, not all. Only an initial few. The scoop is not yet lifting the base; it's merely inserting itself in place."

"What will the ascent rate be?" he asked.

"That hasn't been decided. Look—we're not ready for that; you're talking about ascent rate while we're still involved in getting the scoop in place. This isn't your field; you have no knowledge about dredging. The scoop is moving horizontally at the rate of six inches per twenty-six-hour day, which is virtually not moving at all."

He said, "There's something you don't want me to see."

"Paranoia," Mali said.

Flashing his bifocal light-source to the right of the scoop he made out something, a dense and opaque mass that soared up high, becoming a triangle of planes past which fish swam and onto which barnacles and bivalves and a host of unipodular mollusks and Crustacea clung. And, next to it, where the scoop slowly worked, an identical shape: Heldscalla.

"That's what you didn't want me to see," he said to Mali.

Two cathedrals.

12

"One of them," he said, "is black. The Black Cathedral."

"Not the one they're dredging," Mali said.

"Is he sure?" Joe said. "Could he make such a mistake?" It would kill Glimmung; he knew that intuitively. It would be the end of everything. And of them all. Merely knowing that it existed, and seeing it—he felt the sting of death; ice settled over his heart and remained there. Hopelessly he flashed his torch about, here and there. As if trying to find—and failing to find—a way out.

"You now know," Mali said, "why I wanted to go back up."

He said, "I'll go up with you." He did not want to remain here any longer. Like Mali, he yearned for the surface, for the world above water. That world contained nothing like this . . . and, he thought, it never should. That was never intended. "Let's go," he said to Mali, and swam upward; with each passing second he was farther up from these black-chilled depths and all that they held. "Give me your hand." He turned, reached back for her . . .

And then he saw it. Saw the pot. In the rays of his torch.

"What's wrong?" Mali said in alarm; he had ceased rising.

"I have to go back," he said.

"Don't let it draw you down! That's the terrible thing it does; its valence works on you. *Climb*." She tore her hand away from his and, kicking vigorously, ascended past him, toward the surface above. Her legs kicked as if she were trying to shake loose some binding substance, something which mired her down here.

"You go on up," Joe said. He sank, lower and lower, his eyes never leaving the pot. And steadily he focused his torch on it. It had coral around it, but, for the most part, it remained uncovered. As if, he thought, it was here waiting for me. Trying to ensnare me, the best possible way . . . through the thing I love most.

Mali hesitated above him, then reluctantly descended until she was parallel with him. "What—" she began, and then she, too, saw the pot; she gasped.

"It's a volute krater," Joe said. "Very large." Already he could distinguish colors emanating from it toward him, the colors which bound him more firmly to this spot than all the cords and seaweed, all the other snares. He sank. And sank some more.

"What can you tell about it?" Mali asked. They had almost reached the pot; Joe's arms extended themselves as if acting on their own will. "Is it—"

"Not earthenware," Joe said. "It's been fired past five hundred degrees centigrade. It may even have been fired at a temperature as high as twelve hundred and fifty degrees. There's a great deal of vitrification over and above the glaze." Now he touched it. Carefully he tugged at it. But the coral held it tight. "Stoneware," he decided. "Not porcelain; it's not translucent. The white of the glaze makes me think—as a guess—that it's a stannic oxide compound. If so it would then be a majolica ceramic piece. Tin-enameling, it's generally called. Like the Delft ceramic offerings." He rubbed the surface of the pot. "From the feel, I'd say it's sgraffito ware, with a lead glaze. See? The pattern has been incised through the slip, disclosing the body color beneath. As I say, this is a volute krater . . . but with it here we can probably expect to find psykters and amphoras as well; it's just a question of removing the coral deposits and seeing what's below."

Is it a good pot?" Mali asked. "I mean, to me it looks unique; I think it's terribly pretty. But in your expert opinion—"

"It's superb," he said, simply. "The red glaze is probably from reduced copper; it passed through a reducing atmosphere in the kiln. And ferrous iron. Look at the black. And the yellow, of course, is obtained from antimony. Which produces an excellent yellow." The color of glaze, he reflected, which attracts me the most. The yellows, the blues. I will never change.

He thought, It's almost as if someone put this here for me to find. He rubbed the surface, on and on, appreciating it by tactile sense-impressions, rather than sight. Cupric oxide blues, he said to himself. This pot has everything but that. Did Glimmung have this put here? he asked himself.

To Mali he said, "Has coral been removed from this? Recently? It seems strange it wasn't completely covered."

For a time Mali poked about the pot, examining its surface and that of the coral holding it from below. As she did so he studied the design on the pot. A complex and ornate scene, more ornate even than the *istoriato* style of Urbino. What did the scene show? He studied it, pondering. Not all of the design was visible. And yet—he was accustomed to filling in missing segments removed from pottery pieces. What does this tell? he asked himself. A story, but of what? He peered.

"I don't like the amount of black on it," Mali said, all at once. "Anything black down here undermines my sense of security." She floated away from the pot, her examination over. "Now can we go back up?" she asked. Her tension had become even greater; it grew with each tick of the clock. "I'm not going to stay down here and extinguish my life voluntarily for one damn dumb pot. Pots just aren't that important."

Joe said, "What did your examination show?"

"Coral has been stripped from it within the last six months." She broke a section of coral away, revealing more of the pot. "I can finish the job in a few minutes, when I have my tools."

Now he saw more of the design. The first panel showed a man seated alone in a bleak and empty room. The next, an intersystem spacecraft of commercial design. The third showed a man—evidently the same man—fishing; it showed him lifting a huge black fish from the water. That was where the black glaze which Mali objected to came in: the enormous fish. The next panel he could not see. Coral blocked his view. But something came after the lifting up of the giant black fish. Lifting the fish was not the end. There was at least one more panel and perhaps two.

"This is a flambé glaze," Joe said absently. "As I said before, of reduced copper. But in some places it looks almost like 'dead leaf' glaze; if I didn't know better I'd—"

"You pedantic fop," Mali said savagely. "You miserable nitwit. I'm going up." She kicked away, rose, unfastened the cable which connected them, and was soon gone, her torch flashing above him. He found himself alone with the pot and the nearby Black Cathedral. Silence. And the utter abstention of activity. No fish moved near him; they seemed to shun the Black Cathedral and its environs. They are wise, he decided. As is Mali.

He took one last, long, lonely look at the dead structure, the cathedral which had never been alive.

Bending over the pot he took hold with both hands and tugged mightily, his torch temporarily put aside. The pot broke into many pieces; the pieces drifted away in the ocean currents and he found himself gazing down at the few still-imprisoned fragments.

Bracing himself he grasped a remaining fragment and tore it forward, where the whole pot had been. The consolidated coral hung back; it kept its seizure of the fragment active. And then, by degrees, the coral released the fragment. It came loose in his hands, and at once he flailed for the surface above.

He held in his hand the remaining two panels of the visual narrative. They ascended with him, held tight.

Presently he broke through to the surface. He slid aside his mask, and floating about, examined the two panels by torch light.

"What is it?" Mali called, swimming toward him with long, lean strokes.

"The rest of the pot," he said raspingly.

The first panel showed the great black fish swallowing the man who had caught it. The second—and final—panel revealed the great fish once again. This time it devoured and absorbed a Glimmung . . . or rather *the* Glimmung. Both the man and Glimmung disappeared down the throat of the fish, to be decomposed within its stomach. The man and Glimmung ceased. Only the great black fish remained. It had engulfed all.

"This potsherd—" he began, and then broke off. There was something that he had failed to see at first glance. That something now gathered his attention; it tugged at him, drawing him restlessly, impotently toward it.

In the latter panel a talk balloon had been incised above the fish's head. Words filled the talk balloon, words in his own language. He read them haltingly as he bobbed about upon the uneasy water.

Life on this planet is under water, not on the land. Do not get involved with the fat fake calling himself Glimmung. The depths draw from the earth, and within those depths the real Glimmung can be found.

And then, in very small letters, these words at the edge of the terminal panel.

This has been a public-service message.

"It's insane," Joe said, as Mali swam up beside him. He felt like dropping the fragment of pot, letting it drift down and down into the dark, heavy water, out of sight once more.

Peering over his shoulder, clinging roundly and wetly to him, Mali read the contents of the talk balloon. "Good god," she said, and laughed. "It's like that what is it you have on Earth. Cookies. With messages in them."

"Fortune cookies," Joe said savagely.

"I read where someone in a Chinese restaurant on Earth, in the city San Francisco, opened a fortune cookie and the slip said, 'Abstain from fornication.' " Again she laughed, a warm, throaty laugh; at the same time she clutched at his shoulder, turning herself about so that she faced him. Now all at once she became calm. And very serious. "It's going to make a terrible fight," she said. "To keep the cathedral down there."

Joe said, "*It* doesn't want to come up. The cathedral—it wants to stay down there. This shard is a part of it." He dropped the fragment of pot and at once it sank into oblivion below him; he watched for a second, saw only ebbing water, and then turned back toward Mali once again. "That was the cathedral talking to us," he said. It was a somber thought, a thought he did not like.

"Didn't the pot belong to the Black—"

"No," he said. "Not from the Black one." It had to be faced by all of them, himself, the others, and—Glimmung. "I don't think he knows," Joe said aloud. "It's not merely a question of the Book of the Kalends, what they write as fate. It's not a problem in hydraulic engineering either."

"The soul," Mali said faintly.

"What?" he demanded, with anger.

"I guess I don't mean that," Mali said after a pause.

"You're damn right you don't," Joe said. "Because it's not alive." Despite the message on the potsherd, he said to himself. It's the semblance of life only. Inertia. Like any physical object it remains where it's at until enough force is brought to bear against it . . . and then it moves, reluctantly. Below us, he thought, that cathedral contains a mass of infinite enormity, and we will break ourselves trying to move it. We will never recover, none of us, Glimmung included. And—

It will remain down there, he thought. As it is now. World without end, he thought, as they say in the church. But what a strange cathedral, he thought, to scratch messages on coral-encrusted pots. There must be a better way by which it can communicate to us up here, we who live on the land. And yet . . . Glimmung's way of communicating, his note bobbing around in the water closet of a toilet on Earth . . . that had been equally bizarre. A planetwide propensity, he decided. An ethnic custom, probably sanctioned down through centuries.

Mali said, "It knew you would find that pot."

"How?"

"In the Book of the Kalends. Buried somewhere in a footnote halfway through, in squirrel agate type."

"But for example they were wrong," Joe said, "when they said I would find something in Heldscalla that would cause me to kill Glimmung. So it could only be a guess, and maybe a bad one." Yet, he thought, it did work out. I did find the pot.

And maybe someday, he thought, the tidal currents of reality will sweep Glimmung and me along so that, at last, I kill him. If enough time elapses. In fact, he reflected, if enough time passes everything will happen. Which in a sense was the way the Kalends' Book worked.

Worked—and did not work.

Probability, Joe said to himself. A science in itself. Bernoulli's Theorem, the Bayes-Laplace theorem, the Poisson

Distribution, Negative Binomial Distribution . . . coins and cards and birthdays, and at last random variables. And, hanging over it all, the brooding specter of Rudolf Carnap and Hans Reichenbach, the Vienna Circle of philosophy and the rise of symbolic logic. A muddy world, in which he did not quite care to involve himself. In spite of the fact that it pertained immediately to the Book of the Kalends. Muddier by far than the water realm which lapped at him and Mali.

"Let's get back to the installation," Mali said, and shivered. She abruptly paddled off, leaving him; he saw, ahead of her, the lights which the robot Willis had previously turned on for their benefit. Those lights still burned; the robot waited for them.

Amalita did not get us, Joe reflected as the two of them paddled toward the staging center with its blaze of lights. And for that he was thankful. It had been as awful as Willis—and Mali—had said. His own corpse . . . he could still see, in his mind, the exposed jawbone as it waggled, white and dead in the current of the Aquatic Sub-World. Amalita's world, with its own laws. Filled with refuse and everything half dead.

He reached the illuminated staging area with its three hermetically sealed domes. And there was Willis, waiting to help him up.

The robot seemed irritable as Joe and Mali removed their diving gear. "It's about time, Sir and Lady," Willis said fussily as it gathered up their equipment. "You disobeyed me and stayed too long." It corrected itself. "Disobeyed Glimmung, I mean."

Joe said, "What's the matter with you?"

"Oh, a goddam radio station," Willis said; now it worked with Mali's oxygen tanks. Its strong hands lifted them without effort. "Just consider this." It stripped her suit from her, gathered up everything, and began to lug it toward the supply locker. "I'm sitting here waiting for you to come up and listening to the radio. They're playing Beethoven's 'Ninth.'

Then there's a commercial for a hernia belt. Then the Good
Friday music from Wagner's *Parsifal*. Then an ad for an oint-
ment that cures athlete's foot. Then a chorale from the Bach
cantata *Jesu Du Meine Seele*. Then an ad for a rectal sup-
pository used in the treatment of piles. Then Pergolesi's *Sta-
bat Mater*. Then an ad for a false-teeth dentifrice. Then the
'Sanctus' from the Verdi *Requiem*. Then a laxative ad. Then
the 'Gloria' section from Haydn's *Mass in Time of War*. Then
an ad for an analgesic used for female monthly disorders.
Then a chorale from the *Saint Matthew Passion*. Then an ad
for cat litter. Then—" Abruptly the robot ceased speaking.
It tilted its head, as if listening.

And now Joe heard it. And, beside him, Mali seemed to
have heard it, too; she turned swiftly, then loped to the
building's entrance. Outside, in the meager light, she peered
up.

He followed after her. So did Willis.

A huge bird hung in the night sky, containing two hoops:
one of water, one of fire. Within the two an adolescent female
face gazed out, partially covered by its Paisley shawl. Glimmung, as he had first appeared to Joe, yet now elevated into
an enormous bird form. An eagle, Joe thought wonderingly.
Screaming as it came, ploughing up the nocturnal sky with
its talons. He moved backward a space, into the security of
the building's doorway. And still the great bird soared toward
them, the right-angle hoops spinning with shrill intensity.

"It's the old fellow," Willis said, showing no anxiety. "I
asked him to come. Or did he ask me? I forget. Anyhow the
two of us conversed, but it's a little blurred, now, in my mind.
We have that problem, my colleagues and I."

Mali said, "He's landing."

The bird came to rest in the air, its beak working in spastic
agitation; the yellow eyes glowered at Joe—specifically at Joe
and no one else—and then from the huge craw of the bird,
words came, shouted into the darkness of the night. Words
sharp and wild, a screech of interrogation. *"You,"* the bird

yelled at him. "I didn't want you to go into the ocean. I didn't want you to see what's there, buried at the bottom. You are here to cure pots. What did you see? What did you do?" The shrieks of the bird had a frantic quality about them, an overpowering urgency. Glimmung had come here because he could not wait to find out; he had to know at once what had happened at the ocean bottom.

"I found a pot," Joe said.

"The pot lied!" Glimmung shrieked. "Forget what it said; listen to me instead. Do you understand?"

Joe said, "The pot only told me—"

"There're a thousand lying pots down there," Glimmung broke in. "Each has a separate, false tale to tell to anyone who happens to come by and notice it."

"A great black fish," Joe said. "It showed that."

"There is no fish. Nothing is real down there except Held-scalla. I can bring it up any time; I can do it alone, with no help from you or from anyone. I can bring each pot up myself; I can free them one by one from the coral, and if they break I can repair them or get someone who can. Shall I send you back to your cubicle to play your game? To deteriorate over the years? To sink into decay gradually over the years until you become debris, without mind or plans? Is that what you want?"

"No," Joe said. "That's not what I want."

"You are going back to Terra," Glimmung shrilled; the beak snapped open and shut, open and shut, biting the air savagely.

"I'm sorry I—" Joe began, but the bird cut him off with ruthless fury. And, as before, with overwhelming agitation.

"I will return you to the crate in my basement," Glimmung declared. "You can stay there until the police catch up with you. Further, I will tell them where you are; they will get you and they will reduce you to tatters. Do you understand? Didn't it occur to you that if you disobeyed me I'd expel you? I have no use for you. As far as I am concerned you no longer exist. I'm sorry to yell at you this way, but this is the way I get when I'm thoroughly teed off. You'll have to excuse me."

Joe said, "It seems to me you're going overboard. What in fact have I done? I went below; I found a pot; I—"

"You found the pot I didn't want you to see." The frigid eyes of the bird bored relentlessly, stultifyingly down at him. "Don't you see what you've done? *You've forced my hand.* I have to react *now;* I can't wait!" All at once the bird wheeled upward, spinning and realigning itself, turned now toward the sea, rather than Joe. The bird shot outward, at tremendous velocity; its massive wings flapped with violent rage and the bird soared, rose, and hovered. It hung in the sky above the sea, shrieking in wild, determined bursts of ear-piercing noise. "Cavorting Cary Karns and his six phones won't help you now!" the bird shrilled as it hung in the dark sky, merging with the fog which rolled in, like waves, above the ocean surface. "The radio audience doesn't know about you! The radio audience doesn't care about you!" The bird wheeled, dropped lower . . .

Something rose from the sea.

13

"Oh god," Mali said, standing close to Joe. "It's the Black One. Coming to meet him."

From the sea the Black Glimmung ascended, meeting the authentic Glimmung in midair. Feathers flew in all directions as the two creatures raked each other with their claws; then, almost at once, the tangled mass of the two of them dropped like a stone into the water. On the surface they thrashed momentarily, and it seemed to Joe—unless it was an illusion—that the authentic Glimmung was struggling to extricate himself.

Both Glimmungs disappeared. Out of sight, into the depths of Mare Nostrum.

"It pulled him under," Mali whispered in a stricken voice.

To the robot, Joe said, "Is there anything we can do? To help him? To get him free?" He's drowning, Joe realized. This will kill him.

"He will emerge," the robot said.

"You can't be sure of that," Joe said; Mali, beside him, echoed his words. "Has this ever happened before?" Joe demanded. "Glimmung pulled under?" Instead of lifting

Heldscalla up, he realized, Glimmung had been dragged down . . . to join the Black Glimmung and the Black Cathedral forever. Like *my* corpse; a lifeless thing floating about in the form of mere debris. Dwelling in a box.

"I can fire an HB cartridge into the water," the robot said. "But a warhead like that would kill him, too."

"No," Mali said emphatically.

"This did happen once before," Willis said, reflecting. "In Terran time—" It calculated. "Late in 1936. About the time of the summer Olympics, held in Berlin, that year."

Mali said, "And he made it back up?"

"Yes, Mrs. Lady," Willis answered. "And the Black One slid back down to the bottom again. Where it has remained until now. By coming here, Glimmung took a calculated risk; he knew it might disturb the Black One. That's why he said, 'You've forced my hand.' You did. It's been forced; he's down there now."

Flashing his torch out onto the water, Joe saw something bobbing about. An object which reflected light. "Do you have a power boat?" he asked Willis.

"Yes, Mr. Sir," the robot said. "Do you want to go out there? What if they come boiling up?"

"I want to see what that is out there," Joe said. He already had a good idea.

Grudgingly, the robot went off in search of the boat.

A few minutes later the three of them put-putted their way out onto the dark and turbulent surface of Mare Nostrum.

"There it is," Joe said. "A few yards to the right." He held the object fixed with his torch as the boat approached it. Reaching out, he groped for the thing; his fingers closed over its handle and he lifted it back, into the boat.

A large bottle. And, in the bottle, a note.

"Another message from Glimmung," Joe said acidly as he unscrewed the lid of the bottle and dumped the note out; it fluttered onto the bottom of the boat and he retrieved it carefully. Holding it in the light of the torch he read it.

Watch this place for hourly progress reports. Cordially, Glimmung. P.S. If I'm not up by morning, notify everybody that the Project has been scrubbed. Get back to your own planets as best you can. My best to you all. G.

"Why does he do this?" Joe asked the robot. "Why does he leave notes in bottles and reach people via radio programs and—"

"An idiosyncratic method of interpersonal communication," the robot answered as they put-putted back toward the staging center. "As long as I've known him he's dribbled out opaque, elliptical chunks of information in indirect ways. In your opinion, how ought he to communicate? By satellite?"

"He might as well," Joe said, and felt gloom descend over him in a morbid, taciturn cloud. He withdrew silently into himself; shivering with cold he awaited their arrival back at the staging area.

"He's going to die," Mali said quietly.

"Glimmung?" Joe asked.

She nodded. In the dim light her face seemed ghostly; across it vague shadows flitted, like ebbing tides.

"Did I ever tell you about The Game?" Joe said.

"I'm sorry; at this moment I—"

"It works this way. You take a book title, preferably one well known, and you feed it orally into a computer in Japan, which translates it into Japanese. Then you—"

"Is that what you're going back to?" Mali asked.

"Yes it is," he said.

"I should feel sorry for you," Mali said. "But I can't. You brought this on all of us—you've destroyed Glimmung, who meant to save you from your puerile pastimes. He meant to restore the dignity of work to you in a heroic enterprise, a joint enterprise involving hundreds of us, from a multitude of planets."

"But Mr. Sir had to go below," the robot said.

"Exactly," Mali said.

"The Book of the Kalends made me do it," Joe said.

"No it didn't," the robot said. "You had it in your mind to go below Mare Nostrum before the Kalend showed up and got you to read that passage in The Book."

"A man must do what aids his humanity," Joe said.

"What does that mean?" Mali demanded.

"A figure of speech," Joe said lamely. "What I mean is: like with the mountain climbers . . . it is there." And now, he thought, I have killed Glimmung, as The Book foretold. The Kalend was right. The Kalends are always right. Glimmung is dying as we sit here in this boat, put-putting back to the staging area. Without me, without my descent into Mare Nostrum, he would be alive and functioning. They are right. It's my fault—as Glimmung himself said, there at the end, before the Black Glimmung rose from the sea to do battle with him.

"How do you feel, Joe Fernwright?" Mali asked him. "Knowing what you did, knowing what you are responsible for?"

"Well," Joe said, "I suggest we keep watching the hourly progress reports." It sounded weak even to him; as he said it his voice faded away, ebbed at last into silence. The three of them continued on, no one speaking, until they reached the dock of the staging area and Willis was securing the boat.

" 'The hourly progress reports,' " Mali said sardonically as they climbed up onto the wharf. The bright lights of the staging area blazed around them, giving Mali and Willis an unnatural cast, a kind of blanched-lead aspect, as if they were mimicking human life in a macabre, unnatural way. Or, he thought, as if I've killed them, too, and these are their corpses. But a robot, he decided, does not have a corpse. It's the lighting and the fact that I'm tired. He had never felt such exhaustion in his life; as he climbed he wheezed for air, his lungs aching. It was as if he had tried, by his own muscles, to lift Glimmung out of the sea and back onto dry land—and safety.

Which, he thought, Glimmung deserves.

"It's an interesting story," Joe said, to change the subject, "about how Glimmung first contacted me. I was sitting in my cubicle, with nothing to do, and the mail light lit up. I pressed the button, and down the pipe came—"

"Look," Mali interrupted quietly; her voice was low but deeply intense. She pointed out over the water, and Joe turned his torch in that direction. "It's frothing. From the struggle underneath. The Black Glimmung swallows Glimmung; the Black Cathedral swallows the cathedral; Amalita and Borel are forgotten, and so is Glimmung. Nothing survives; nothing comes back up out of the water." She turned her back and continued on into the staging area.

"Just a moment," the robot said. "I think a call is coming through for Mr. Sir. As before, an official call." The robot became silent and then it said, "Glimmung's personal secretary. She wants to talk to you once again." The door of the robot's chest swung open and, as before, on its tray appeared the audio telephone. "Please pick up the receiver," the robot instructed.

Once again Joe picked up the receiver. He felt weights, attached to his arms, drag him down; he had to struggle to hold the receiver up high enough so that he could hear.

"Mr. Fernwright?" The professional, adequate, female voice. "This is Hilda Reiss, again. Is Glimmung there with you?"

"Tell her," Mali said. "Tell her the truth."

Joe said, "He's at the bottom of Mare Nostrum."

"Is that so, Mr. Fernwright? Do I understand you correctly?"

"He went down into the Aquatic Sub-World," Joe said. "All of a sudden. None of us expected it."

"I don't think I'm understanding you properly," Miss Reiss said. "You seem to be saying—"

"He's fighting with everything he's got," Joe said. "I'm sure he'll emerge eventually. He says he'll be sending up hourly progress reports. So I don't think there's really too much to worry about."

"Mr. Fernwright," Miss Reiss said briskly, "Glimmung only sends out hourly progress reports when he's in distress."

"Hmm," Joe said.

"Do you understand me?" Miss Reiss snapped.

"Yes." Joe nodded.

"Did he go under voluntarily or was he dragged under?"

"A little bit of both," Joe said. "There was a confrontation." He gesticulated, finding it difficult to bring forth the right words. "Between the two of them. But Glimmung decidedly seemed to have the upper hand. Or should I say pseudopodium?"

"Let me talk to her," Mali said; she seized the phone, tugged it from his hand, and spoke into it. "This is Miss Yojez." An interval of silence. "Yes, Miss Reiss; I know that. Yes, I know that, too. Well, as Mr. Fernwright says, he may emerge victorious. We must have faith, as the Bible says." Again a prolonged period of listening. Then she glanced up at Joe, held her hand over the mouthpiece of the phone, said, "She wants us to try to get a message down to Glimmung."

"What message?" Joe said.

Into the phone Mali said, "What message?"

"No message," Joe said to Willis, "is going to be of any help to him. There isn't anything we can do." He felt utterly impotent, more so than at any other time of his life. The sense of the proximity of death, which had haunted him during his depressed periods, dilated in him, and in undismayed fury; he felt it numb his guts, his heart, his nervous system. Awareness of guilt clung to him like a satin, ornate cloak. Shame so pure that it had virtually an archetypal quality to it, as if he were reexperiencing the primordial shame of Adam, the first sense of conspicuousness before the sight of God. He felt hatred for himself, for the fecklessness of his conduct; he had brought his benefactor into jeopardy— and the entire planet as well. I'm a Jonah, he said to himself. The Kalends are right; I have come here to blight this planet with my presence. And Glimmung must have known . . . yet, he brought me here anyhow. Perhaps because I needed this; for my sake. Christ, he thought. And this is now the end. Look how I've paid him back: with death.

Mali hung up the phone. Her face, strained and taut, moved until she confronted Joe Fernwright directly; she gazed at him without blinking for a long, long time. She gazed at him with fire-swollen intensity, and then, spent, she shuddered and ducked her head down, as if swallowing. "Joe," she said huskily, "Miss Reiss says for us to give up. To leave here and go back to the Olympia Hotel for our things. And then—" She paused, her face knotting profoundly. "And then leave Plowman's Planet and return to our own worlds."

"Why?" Joe said.

"Because there's no hope. And once Glimmung is—" She made a convulsive gesture. "Is dead, then the scourge will descend on everybody on the planet. So we should get . . . you know . . . *out*."

Joe said, "But the note in the bottle said to watch for hourly progress reports."

"There will be no progress reports."

"Why not?"

She said nothing; she did not amplify.

Chilled with fear, Joe said, "Is she going to leave?"

"Yes, but first Miss Reiss will be staying behind to route everybody to the spaceport. There's an intersystem ship that can begin loading at any time. She hopes to have everyone on it within the next hour." To Willis, Mali said, "Call me a taxi."

"You have to say, 'Willis, call me a taxi,' " the robot said.

"Willis, call me a taxi."

"You're leaving?" Joe asked. He felt surprise and, in addition, a further sinking of his life sense.

"We've been told to," Mali said simply.

Joe said, "We've been told to watch for hourly progress reports."

"You damn fool," Mali said.

"I intend to stay here," Joe said.

"All right, stay here." To Willis she said, "Did you call for a cab?"

"You have to say—"

"Willis, did you call for a cab?"

"They're all busy," the robot said. "Shuttling people from every corner of this rusty old world of ours to the spaceport."

Joe said, "Let her have the vehicle you and I came here in."

"Then you're sure you don't intend to leave?" the robot asked.

"I'm sure," Joe said.

"I think I can follow your reasoning," Mali said. "It was you who made this come about, this trouble crisis. So you feel it would be immoral to leave, to save yourself."

"No," he said. Truthfully, he said, "I'm too tired. I can't face going back home. I'll take a calculated risk. If Glimmung returns to dry land then we can continue with the raising of Heldscalla. If not—" He shrugged.

"Fake bravery," Mali said.

"Fake nothing. Just weariness. Get going; take off for the spaceport. The end could come any minute, as you well know."

"Well, anyhow that's what Miss Reiss told me," Mali said, somewhat apologetically. She loitered, clearly divided in her mind as to what to do. "If I stay—" she began, but Joe cut her off.

"You're not staying. You and everyone else. Except me."

"May I interpose a point?" Willis inquired. Neither of them replied, so it continued. "It was never Glimmung's intention that anyone die with him. Hence Miss Reiss's instructions to all of you; she is following his dictates. Undoubtedly he left a standing order with her that if he were killed she would get everyone off the planet, hopefully in time. Do you see, Mr. Sir?"

"I see," Joe said.

"Then you'll leave with Miss Lady?"

"No," Joe said.

"Terrans are known for their stupidity," Mali said scathingly. "Willis, drive me to the spaceport direct; I'll leave my things in my apartment. Let's go."

"Goodby, Mr. Sir," Willis said to Joe.

"Rots of ruck," Joe said.

"What does that mean?" Mali demanded.

"Nothing. An archaic drollery." He walked away from the two of them, to the wharf; standing there he gazed sightlessly down at the moored boat, and, in it, the bottle and note. Rots of ruck to me, too, he thought. "It was never a very good drollery anyhow," he said to no one in particular. To Glimmung, he thought. Luck to him. Down in Mare Nostrum, where I ought to be. Where we all should be. Fighting, as he is fighting, the Black Entities that have never lived. Death on the move, he thought; animated death. Death with an appetite.

He said aloud, " 'Cursed with an appetite keen I am.' "

They had gone. He stood alone in the staging center. And, presently, he heard rockets, a low murmur of power that shook the building: they had taken off.

"From *Princess Ida*," he said, to no one. "Sung by Cyril, in act two, in the gardens of Castle Adamant." He was silent, then, listening. He could no longer hear rockets. What a hell of a thing, he thought. A really lousy hell of a thing. And I brought it on. The Book made a pool ball out of me, an object set in motion, as in Aristotle's view of the world. One moving pool ball hits the next; it hits a third; that is the essence of life.

Would Mali and Willis have known what he was quoting from? Mali no . . . but Willis was familiar with Yeats. Surely it would be equally familiar with W. S. Gilbert. Yeats. He then thought this:

Q. Do you like Yeats?

A. I don't know, I've never tried any.

For a time his mind was empty and then he thought this:

Q. Do you like Kipling?

A. I don't know, I've never kippled.

Anguish and despair filled him as these thoughts passed through his brain. I've gone mad, he said to himself. Only rubbish occupies my attention; I am flattened by pain. What is going on down there?

He stood on the dock, gazing out across the water. Firm and smooth—the surface hid anything beneath; he could get no idea from what he saw, no understanding. And then—

A quarter mile from the staging area the water began violently to churn. Something huge rose to the surface, thrashed about, and then tore itself loose. The vast object spread wings which beat ineffectually; the wings continued beating, slowly, as if the creature were exhausted. And then, in a ragged, careening flight, the thing rose up. It pumped its wings up and down, and yet it did not rise more than a few feet from the surface.

Glimmung? He strained to see as the thing drew closer; it pumped and flapped until it reached a dome of the staging area. It did not land, however; laboriously it continued past; he heard and felt it go by overhead in the night's darkness.

At the same time an autonomic alarm, triggered by the

thing's proximity, tripped on; a recorded, stentorian voice began to speak from horns here and there throughout the structure.

"Attention! A false Glimmung is active! Take emergency procedures under condition Three! Attention! A false Glimmung—" It boomed on and on.

The flailing, thrashing object which had risen from the sea was not Glimmung.

14

The worst alternative had come about. Glimmung had been defeated. He realized it as he heard the alarm and listened to the heavy rustle of giant, preoccupied wings. The thing had a mission. It was heading in a calculated direction. Where? Joe wondered. Reflexively he cringed; even without landing it cast its terrible weight over the planet's surface. And over him as well. It seemed as if he bore the thing, at least momentarily. It's not interested in me, he said to himself, as he crouched, eyes shut, his body drawn into a fetal position.

He said aloud, "Glimmung."

There was no answer.

It's heading toward the spaceport, he said to himself. They will never leave this planet. Going that way—he sensed the determination in its exhausted straining. Glimmung had damaged it but not destroyed it. And Glimmung lay at the bottom of Mare Nostrum, probably—almost certainly—dying.

I've got to go below, Joe realized. I have to dive once more, to see if there's anything I can do for him. Frantically, he began collecting his previous diving gear; he found oxygen tanks, the transparent mask, flippers, his torch; he located weights to fix his belt . . . feverishly he worked. And, as he crept into the skintight suit, he realized that it didn't matter. He was too late.

And, he thought, even if I find him I have no way of grappling him; I have no hoist by which to bring him up. And who can heal him? Not me. Not anyone.

He gave up. He began stripping the suit and weighted belt from him. His half-paralyzed fingers plucked at the zipper—the job of desuiting lay almost beyond his capacity.

A disaster of a trade, he thought. Glimmung now on the ocean bottom; the Black Glimmung, the false Glimmung, in charge of the sky. Everything has been reversed, and a dangerous situation has become a catastrophe.

But at least, he thought, it didn't try to get me. It flapped on past . . . in search of greater prey.

He gazed out across the water; he shone his torch on the spot where Glimmung and his antithesis had sunk. What appeared to be bits of hide and broken clumps of feathers shone pale and sticky in the light of the torch. And a deep stain eddying out in greater and greater circles like oil. Blood, he thought. The thing is hurt, all right. Unless that's Glimmung's blood.

Stiffly, his arms shaking, he managed to creep down into the moored power boat. Presently he had put-putted out to the spot; the blood slick glistened on all sides of his boat as he shut off the power to the engine and merely drifted. The flotsam told him nothing. Even so, he remained there, listening to the sound of waves flopping blindly against a dark coastline somewhere behind him. Experimentally, he reached his hand down into the water and brought it out. The slime, in torch light, looked black. But it was blood. Fresh blood and lots of it. Blood from something which had been permanently maimed. Beyond hope of recovery.

It—whoever lost this blood—will die in a matter of days, he decided. Or possibly hours.

From the depths of the ocean a bottle floated up. At once he spotted it with his torch, snapped the power on to the engine, and put-putted toward it; reaching, he lifted the bottle into the boat.

A note. He uncorked the bottle, shook the note out into his waiting hand. By torch light he read it.

Good news! I have routed the opposition and am presently recuperating.

In disbelief he reread the words. Is it a gag? he wondered. Fake bravado at a time like this? And that was exactly what the pot had called Glimmung: *a fake*. And, by extension, the note itself a forgery, not really from Glimmung; like the words on the pot, this could be a product of the cathedral—not the Black counterpart but by the Heldscalla which Glimmung intended—or had intended—to raise. "I have routed the opposition," he echoed in his mind as he reread the note once again. There is a credibility gap here, he decided. The enemy, as it thrashed its way out of the water and into the air, had seemed damaged but not mortally so. It was Glimmung, unable to ascend from the ocean floor, who seemed to Joe to be mortally damaged, despite this note.

A second bottle, smaller than the previous two, floated to the surface. He sequestered it, unscrewed the lid, and read the brief note within.

The previous communiqué is not a forgery. I am in good health and hope you are the same. G.
P.S. It will no longer be necessary for anyone to leave the planet. Notify them that I am all right, and tell them to stay in their living areas for the time being. G.

"But it's too late," Joe said aloud. They're leaving right now. Glimmung, you waited too long. I am the only one left. I and the robots; in particular Willis. And we are not much.

Nothing at all compared with the gigantic and varied crew which you assembled for the task of raising Heldscalla. Your Project has come to an end.

And what was more this note could be a forgery, too. An attempt by the cathedral to hold onto everyone, to keep them from leaving the planet as Miss Reiss had ordered. However, the note had the authentic ring of Glimmung's style. If the notes were forgeries, they were good ones.

Taking the last sheet of paper, Joe wrote an answer on the back of it in block letters.

If you are in good health why are you staying down below?
Signed Worried Employee.

He stuffed the note in one of the bottles, put in a weight from his belt, screwed tight the lid, and dropped the bottle over the side of the boat. It sank immediately. And, almost immediately, came bobbing back up. He fished it in and opened it.

I am currently dispatching the Black Cathedral. Will return to the dry land when that has been done. Signed Confident Employer.
P.S. Get the others. They will be needed. G.

Obediently, but without conviction, Joe put-putted back to the lit-up staging area. He located a vidphone—there were several—and when connected asked the autonomic phone system to connect him with the tower at the planet's sole spaceport.

"When did the last major ship take off?" he asked the tower.

"Yesterday."

"Then you have an intersystem ship on your pad right now?"

"Yes, we do."

Good news, and yet, in a sense, ominous news, too. Joe said, "Glimmung wants it halted and the passengers dispersed so that they can come here."

"You have authority to speak for Mr. Glimmung?"

"Yes," Joe said.

"Prove it."

"He told me orally."

"Prove it."

"If you let the ship go," Joe said, "then Heldscalla will never be raised. And Glimmung will destroy you."

"Let's see you verify that."

"Let me talk to Miss Reiss," Joe said.

"Who is Miss Reiss?"

"Aboard the ship. Glimmung's private secretary."

"I can't take orders from her either. I'm autonomic."

"Did a huge flapping thing, completely black, come your way?"

"No."

"Well," Joe said, "it's heading there. It should show up any time. Everyone on board the ship will die because you won't tell them to disperse."

"Neurotic panic alarms cannot dissuade me," the tower said, but it sounded uneasy, now. There was a pause; Joe sensed it straining to see and hear at the farthest reach of its sensory apparatus. "I—" the tower said haltingly. "I think I see it."

"Disperse the ship's passengers," Joe said. "Before it's too late."

"But they'll be sitting hens," the tower said.

"Ducks," Joe corrected.

"My point is clear though the metaphor be wrong," the tower said. But now it sounded uncertain of itself. "Perhaps I could put you through to someone aboard the ship."

"Hurry," Joe said.

The phone's screen showed a variety of unnatural colors, and then upon it there appeared the rugged, gray, massive head of Harper Baldwin. "Yes, Mr. Fernwright?" He, like the tower, showed acute nervousness. "We're just leaving. I understand a false Glimmung is headed this way. Unless we take off immediately—"

"The orders are changed," Joe said. "Glimmung is alive and well and wants you all here at the aquatic staging center. As soon as possible."

A cool, practical, competent face appeared on the vidscreen. A near-female face. "This is Hilda Reiss. In a situation like this our only viable alternative is to evacuate Plowman's Planet; I thought you understood that. I told Miss Yojez—"

"But Glimmung wants you here," Joe said. The red tape; the damn red tape. He held the note from Glimmung before the vidscreen. "You recognize his writing? As his personal, private secretary you should."

She peered, forehead wrinkled. " 'It will no longer be necessary for anyone to leave the planet,' " she read aloud. " 'Notify them that I am all right. And tell them—' "

Joe held the next note before the screen.

" 'Get the others,' " Miss Reiss read. "I see. Well, that is certainly quite distinct." She eyed Joe. "All right, Mr. Fernwright. We will hire werj drivers and vehicles and come to the staging center posthaste. You can expect us in ten or fifteen minutes. For a number of reasons I hope that the false Glimmung let loose will not destroy us on the way. Bye." She rang off, then. The screen became dark, the receiver silent.

Ten minutes, Joe thought. And with the Black Glimmung over their heads. They'll be lucky if they can get any werjes to drive them. Even the autonomic tower, a synthetic construct, had been worried.

The hope of their arriving at the aquatic staging center seemed dim.

•••

Half an hour passed. There was no sign of a hovercraft, no manifestation of the group. It got them, Joe Fernwright said to himself. They are finished. And, meanwhile, Glimmung battles the Black Cathedral at the bottom of Mare Nostrum. Everything is being decided right now.

Why don't they come? he asked himself violently. Did it get them? Are they corpses floating in the water or drying to bleached teeth and bones on the land? And Glimmung. What about him? Even if they get here, everything still depends on Glimmung's victory over the Black Cathedral. If he dies then they have come here for nothing; we will all leave, leave here, leave the planet. Back to overcrowded Earth for me, with phony money, the vets' dole, the empty cubicle where nothing happens. And The Game, the goddam Game. For the remainder of my life.

I'm not going to leave here, he said to himself. Even if Glimmung dies. But—what would this world be like without Glimmung? Ruled by the Book of the Kalends . . . a mechanistic world, each day cranked out by The Book; a world without freedom. The Book will tell us each day what we are going to do, and we will do it. And, eventually, The Book will tell us we are going to die, and we will—

Die. He thought, The Book was wrong; it said what I found down below the surface of the ocean would cause me to kill Glimmung. *And it didn't.*

But Glimmung could still die; the prophecy could still come true. Two battles remain: the battle to destroy the Black Cathedral, and the battle, the terrible task, of lifting Heldscalla to the surface. Glimmung could die during either; he could be dying right now. And all our hopes with him.

He turned on the radio to see if there was any news.

"Impotent?" the radio said. "Unable to achieve an orgasm? Hardovax will turn disappointment into joy." Another voice, then, that of a miserable male. "Gosh, Sally, I don't know what's been the matter with me. I know you've noticed that I'm completely flaccid of late. Gosh, everyone's noticed." A female voice, then. "Henry, what you need is a simple pill called Hardovax. And in days you'll be a real man." " 'Hardovax'?" Henry echoed. "Gosh, maybe I should try it." Then the announcer's voice again. "At your nearby drugstore or write direct to—" Joe shut it off, at that point. Now I know what Willis meant, he said to himself.

A large hovercar landed at the miniature field of the staging center. He heard it arrive; he felt the building quiver and vibrate. So they made it, he said to himself, and hurried toward the field to meet them. His legs felt like heated thermoplastic; he could barely support himself.

Harper Baldwin, tall and stern, emerged first. "There you are, Fernwright." Harper Baldwin shook hands cordially with Joe; he seemed relaxed, now. "It was quite a battle."

"What happened?" Joe said, as the sharp-faced middle-aged woman stepped out. Chrissakes, he thought. Don't just stand there; tell me. "How did you get away from it?" he asked as the reddish, heavyset man emerged, then the matronly woman, and, after her, the timid little fellow.

Mali Yojez, appearing, said, "Calm down, Joe. You get so agitated."

Now the nonhumanoid life-forms made their way from the hovercraft onto the small field. The multilegged gastropod, the immense dragonfly, the furry ice cube, the red jelly supported by its metal frame, the univalvular cephalopod, the kindly looking bivalve Nurb K'ohl Dáq, the quasiarachnid, its chitinous shell gleaming, its many legs drumming . . . and then the portly, rope-tailed werj driver himself. The various forms scuttled, wiggled, walked, and haltingly slithered under the protection of the three hermetically sealed domes of the staging center, getting themselves out of the nocturnal cold. Mali, alone, remained with Joe—except for the werj driver, who loitered nearby, smoking some peculiar form of native grass. It looked pleased with itself.

"Was it that bad?" Joe asked Mali.

Still pale and tense, but, like Harper Baldwin, beginning to unwind, Mali said, "It was awful, Joe."

"And no one is going to talk about it," Joe said.

"I'll talk," Mali said. "Just give me a moment." Holding out her hand to the werj she said, "Just give me a moment." She trembled, then got out a cigarette, smoked rapidly, passed the cigarette to Joe. "When Ralf and I were here we got to using this. I find it helpful." He shook his head no, and Mali nodded. "Let's see." She ruminated. "After your call we got out of the ship. As we were leaving the ship the Black Glimmung approached and began to circle the ship. We hailed this werj and—"

"I took off," the werj said, proudly.

"Yes, it took off," Mali continued. "It was told the situation, fully and completely, in case it didn't want to take us, and it flew almost touching the ground; it flew I would say on an average of ten feet above the nearby buildings and then the open country. And, most important of all, it took a route it was familiar with." To the werj she said, "I forget why you developed that strange anabasis. Explain again."

The werj removed the cigarette from its gray lips and said, "Income-tax violators."

"Yes," Mali said to Joe, nodding. "Plowman's Planet has a huge income tax, roughly seventy percent of earned gross income, as an average . . . it varies, of course, depending on the bracket. You see, the werjes usually drive that route the other way; that is, starting in a distant residential spot and zigzagging, et cetera, to the spaceport, avoiding the native police and tax agents and getting the passenger aboard a ship before he's caught. Once on the ship he's safe, because the ship is recognized as extranational territory, like an embassy."

"I can always get them there," the werj said sleekly. "Onto a ship, before they're caught. No police cruiser, even with radar, can spot me as I zero in on the spaceport. In ten years I've only been stopped once, and that time I was clean." It grinned as it puffed on its cigarette.

Joe said, "You mean the Black Glimmung took off after you?"

"No," Mali said. "It crashed into the ship, a few minutes after we vacated it. The ship was totally destroyed, according to what we heard over the air, and the Black Glimmung was injured."

"Then why did you need an elaborate escape route?" Joe asked, bewildered.

"It seemed like a good idea at the time," Mali said. "I understand from Hilda Reiss that Glimmung is currently attacking the Black Cathedral. Have you heard any further word, since the note Miss Reiss saw over the vidphone?"

"No," Joe said. "I haven't looked; I was waiting for all of you to show up."

"One more minute," Mali said, "aboard that ship, sitting there, waiting for takeoff, and we would have been killed. It was too close, Joe. I wouldn't want to live through it again. I think it thought the ship was alive because the ship was so large. And we were too small; it apparently never saw the hovercar."

"Funny things happen on this planet," the werj said. Now it was picking its teeth with its elongated thumbnail. It all at once held out its hand.

"What do you want?" Joe said. "To shake hands?"

"No," the werj said. "I want .85 of a crumble. They said you'd pay the bill for me bringing them here over my extra-good escape type route."

"Bill Glimmung," Joe said.

"You don't have .85 of a crumble?" the werj asked.

"No," Joe said.

"Do you?" the werj said to Mali.

"None of us has been paid," Mali said. "We'll pay you when Glimmung pays us."

"I could call in the police," the werj said, but fundamentally it appeared to be reconciled. Basically, Joe decided, it's a humble creature. It will let us pay later.

Mali took his arm and led him indoors; the werj remained behind, glowering fruitlessly. But it did not try to halt them. "I think," Mali said, "that we've gained a great victory. I mean by our escape from the Black Glimmung, and its injury; I understand that it's still there at the spaceport, and the authorities are trying to decide what to do with it. They'll wait until Glimmung tells them what they should do. That's the way they've worked for decades, in fact since Glimmung came here. At least that's what Ralf used to say. He was very interested in the way Glimmung ran this planet; he used to say—"

"What if Glimmung does die?" Joe said.

"Then the werj won't get paid," Mali said.

"I'm not thinking about that," Joe said. "I mean this: if Glimmung dies, will the Black Glimmung be patched up and allowed to rule this planet? In his place? As the next best substitute?"

"Lord knows," Mali said. She joined the group, the variegated life-forms from a variety of planets; arms folded, she stood listening to what Harper Baldwin was saying to the kindly bivalve.

"Faust always dies," Harper Baldwin said.

Nurb K'ohl Dáq answered, "Only in Marlowe's play and in the legends which Marlowe drew on."

"Everyone knows that Faust dies," Harper Baldwin said; he surveyed the group of life-forms gathered in a circle around him and the bivalve. "Isn't that true?" he asked them all.

Joe said, "It's not preordained."

"Yes it is!" Harper Baldwin said emphatically. "In the Book of the Kalends. Specifically. Look again. We've lost sight of it; we should have left when we could, when our ship was getting ready to fire off its launch rockets."

"Then we would have died," the quasiarachnid said, its

many arms waving in excitement. "The Black Glimmung would have killed every one of us, the moment it hit our ship."

"That's true," Mali put in.

"Actually that's so," Nurb K'ohl Dáq said, in his kindly way. "We are here only because Mr. Fernwright was able to reach Miss Hilda Reiss and tell us that Glimmung wanted us to evacuate the ship, which we did, and not a moment—"

"Balls," Harper Baldwin said angrily.

Joe picked up his torch and walked from the staging area to the wharf. He shone the helium-powered bright light out onto the surface of dark water, seeking for—something. Anything. Any sign of Glimmung's condition. He examined his watch. Nearly an hour had passed since Glimmung had met the Black Glimmung and had dropped to the floor of Mare Nostrum, to do fatal battle with his Doppelgänger, and, after that, to struggle with the Black Cathedral itself. Is he alive? Joe wondered. Would his corpse float to the surface, or, like mine, would it remain down below in the realm of decay, rotting into offal, hiding in a box or other construct, not alive and yet not totally inert? A kind of semisentient state that might continue for centuries. And—the Black Cathedral would be free to rise to the surface and onto dry land. Once Glimmung is dead then nothing can halt it.

Maybe there was a further note. He searched the water for a bottle; he whisked the light here and there, sweeping out an enormous area.

No bottle. Nothing.

Mali came up beside him. "Anything?"

"No," he said curtly.

"Do you know what I think?" Mali said. "I think, as I've always thought, that he's fated to fail. The Book is right and Harper Baldwin is right. Faust always fails and Glimmung is an incarnation of Faust. The striving, the restless intensity . . . it's all there; the legend is fulfilled, in fact is being fulfilled right now as we stand here."

"Maybe so," Joe said, still lashing the water with shafts of white light.

Mali took his arm and nuzzled close to him. "It's safe, now. We could leave. The Black One isn't after us anymore."

"I'm staying here." Joe moved away from her, still sweeping the water with his torch. No thoughts crossed his mind; mentally he was blank, merely listening passively, waiting. Waiting for a clue, a sign. *Any* sign of what was going on below.

All at once the water stirred. He swung the torch, lit up that general area. He strained to see.

Something enormous was attempting to come to the surface. What was it? Heldscalla? Glimmung? Or—the Black Cathedral? He waited, trembling. The vast object made the water boil and hiss; clouds of steam traveled upward and the night was alive with a full roaring, a cauldron of haste and activity and titanic effort.

Mali said quietly, "It's Glimmung. And he's badly hurt."

15

The hoop of fire had been extinguished. Only one hoop turned, the hoop of water, and it grated piercingly . . . as if, Joe thought, a machine is dying, not a living creature.

The others of the group made their way to the wharf. "He's failed," the red jelly supported by the metal frame said. "You can see; he's beginning to die."

"Yes," Joe said, aloud, and was surprised to hear his own voice; it rang harshly in the midst of the moans rising from the injured Glimmung. Several others in the group echoed his word; it was as if he had pronounced a ban, as if it was his decision to make, whether Glimmung would live or not live. "But we can't be really sure until we get out there," he said. He set down his torch and descended the wooden ladder to the parked boat. "I'm going to go and find out," he said; he reached for his torch and then, squatting and shivering in the chill night wind, started the engine of the boat.

"Don't go," Mali said.

Joe grated, "I'll see you in a little while." He guided the boat from its dock, out into the furiously lapping waves created by the thrashing bulk of Glimmung's body.

An enormity of injury, he thought as the boat rose and fell, put-putting its way anxiously forward. Injury on a scale which we really can't understand. Damn it, he thought with bitterness. Why does it have to end this way? Why couldn't it have been otherwise? He felt numb, as if death were assailing him, too. As if he and Glimmung—

The huge shape wallowed in the water, and, as it lay, blood poured from it; like Christ on the cross it bled eternally, as if its blood supply was infinite. As if, Joe thought, this moment is going to last forever: me in the boat, trying to get close, and him floundering and bleeding and dying. God, he thought; this is awful, truly awful. And yet he guided the boat on, closer and closer.

From the depths of himself Glimmung said, "I—need you. All of you."

"What can we do?" He continued on, closer and closer; now the periphery of the body strained and twisted only a yard from the prow of the boat. Water and blood swamped its way into the boat; Joe felt it sink below him. He gripped the sides, tried to shift his weight. But blood and water continued to pour in. I will be drowned, he thought, in another few seconds.

Reluctantly, he reversed direction; he backed away from Glimmung. The boat ceased taking liquid. And yet he felt no better. His fear and agony remained the same, his empathic identification with his dying employer.

Glimmung sputtered, "I—I—" He slobbered, now, rolling on his side, unable to control the thrashing of his maimed body.

"Whatever it is," Joe said, "we'll do it."

"That's—inordinately receptive—of you," Glimmung managed to whisper, and then he revolved entirely; he sank below the surface, so that speech, for him, became impossible.

The end, Joe thought, has come.

Wretchedly, he turned the boat about and, misery weighing him down, steered for the wharf once more. It was over.

As he tied up the boat, Mali and Harper Baldwin and several nonhumanoids reached to help him.

"Thanks," he said, and clumsily ascended the wooden ladder. "He's dead," Joe said. "Or almost dead. Virtually dead." He let Miss Reiss and Mali sweep a blanket over him, a warm cloak which settled into place over his foam- and blood-drenched body. My god, he realized. I'm soaking wet. He had no memory of it; at the time he had been concerned with what he saw only. With Glimmung. Now he turned his attention on himself . . . and found that he was wet, freezing, and filled with despair.

"Here's a local cigarette," Mali said; she placed it between his trembling lips. "Get inside. Don't watch. There's nothing you can do. You tried."

Joe said, shakily, "He asked for our help."

"I know," Mali said. "We heard him." The others of the group nodded silently, their faces bleached with unyielding pain.

"But I don't know what it is," Joe said. "The help we can do. I don't see anything we can do, but he was trying to say. Maybe if he could have said it we could have done it. The last thing he said, did, was to thank me." He let Mali lead him under the hermetically sealed dome and into the radiant heat of the staging center.

"We'll leave this planet tonight," Mali said presently, as the two of them stood together.

"Okay," he said. He nodded.

"Come to my planet with me," Mali said. "Don't go back to Earth; you'd be so unhappy there."

"Yeah," he agreed. It was true. Beyond any doubt, any possible doubt whatever. As W. S. Gilbert would have put it. "Where's Willis?" he asked, looking around. "I want to trade quotes with him."

"Quotations," Mali corrected.

He nodded in agreement. "Yes," he said. "I meant to say quotations."

"You're really tired."

"Hell," he said, "I don't know why I should be; all I did was paddle out there in a boat to try to talk with him."

"The responsibility," Mali said.

"What responsibility? I couldn't even hear him."

"But the promise you made. Regarding us all."

Joe said, "Anyhow I failed."

"*He* failed. It's not your fault. You were listening—we all were listening. He never managed to say it."

"Is he still on the surface?" Joe asked; he peered past her, across the wharf, at the water beyond.

"He's on the surface, slowly drifting this way."

Joe tossed down the cigarette, ground it out with his heel, and started for the wharf.

"Stay in here," Mali said, trying to stop him. "It's sealed against the cold. You're still wet; you'll die."

"Do you know how Gilbert died?" he asked her. "William Schwenck Gilbert? He had a heart attack trying to rescue a girl who was drowning." He pushed past her, through the thermal barrier, and outdoors onto the wharf once more. "I won't die," he said to her as she followed after him. "Which in a sense is too bad." Maybe it would be more useful, he thought, to die with Glimmung. That way, at least, we could show how we felt. But who would notice? Who is left to notice? Spiddles and werjes, he thought. And robots. He continued on, pushing his way through the group, until he reached the edge of the wharf.

Four torches illuminated the expiring hulk which had once been Glimmung; in their light Joe watched, as the others watched, silently. He could think of no comment, and no comment seemed to be needed. Look at him, he said to himself. And I brought it about. So the Book of the Kalends was right after all; by going down below I caused his death.

"You did it," Harper Baldwin said to him.

"Yep," Joe said stoically.

"Any reason?" the multilegged gastropod lisped.

"No," Joe said. "Unless you want to count stupidity."

"I'm ready to count it," Harper Baldwin rasped.

"Okay," Joe said. "You do that." He looked; he looked; he looked; Glimmung came closer; closer; closer. And then, at the edge of the wharf, almost against it, the body reared up.

"Watch out!" Mali screamed from behind him; the group broke, scattered, hurried toward the security of the hermetically sealed dome.

Too late. Glimmung's bulk descended on the wharf; the wood splintered and sank. Joe, gazing up, saw from outside into the immense body. And then, a moment later, *saw from inside the body out.*

Glimmung had enclosed them. All. No one had escaped, not even the robot Willis, who had stood far off to one side. Caught up, trapped. Included in that which was Glimmung.

He heard Glimmung speak—heard not through his ears but in his brain. And, at the same time, heard the babble of the others, of the remainder of the group; their voices, the unceasing din, muttered beyond Glimmung's own voice, like crosstalk. "Help me? Where am I? Get me out of here!" They babbled against one another, like disturbed, frightened ants. And Glimmung's voice boomed, overpowering but not quenching them. "I have asked you here today," Glimmung declared, bombarding Joe's brain, "because I need your help. Only you can give it to me."

We're a part of him, Joe realized. A part! He tried to see, but his eyes registered only a swirling, jellolike image, a film which obliterated rather than revealed the reality around him. I'm not on the edge, he thought; I'm at the center. So I have no vision. Those at the edge can see, but—

"Please listen to me," Glimmung interrupted, fragmenting his batlike flittering thoughts. "Concentrate. If you do not, you will be absorbed and finally vanish, and hence be of no use to me or to anyone else. I need you to live, as separate entities combined within my one somatic presence."

"Will we ever get out?" Harper Baldwin yammered. "Are we going to have to remain in here forever?"

"I want out!" Miss Reiss cried in panic. "Let me loose!"

"Please," the immense dragonfly implored. "I want to fly and sing; I am held down in here, pushed and compressed and made not alone. Sanction my flight, Glimmung!"

"Free us!" Nurb K'ohl Dáq begged. "This is unfair!"

"You're destroying us!"

"We're being sacrificed for your ends!"

"How can we help you if we're destroyed?"

Glimmung said, "You are not destroyed. You are engulfed."

"That's being destroyed," Joe said.

"No," Glimmung boomed, "it is not." He began to lumber away from the remains of the wharf, the scattered bits of wood which he had not absorbed. Down, Glimmung thought, and the thought impressed itself in Joe's brain—as well as in the other brains around him. Down to the bottom. The time has come; Heldscalla must be raised.

Now, Glimmung thought. What sank down centuries ago will be spewed up, once more, to the surface. Amalita and Borel, he thought. You will be free and on the shore; it will all be as it was before, worlds without end.

Depth. The water became dull. Forms darted or crept by, a multitude of them, no two alike. The snowflakes of the sea, he thought. A winter of vegetable life which crawls over and hangs onto. Let go.

Before him Heldscalla lay. Its pale turrets, its Gothic arch, its flying buttresses, its red-stained glass made from gold— he saw all of it from a dozen eyes. It was intact, except for the engineering divisions, from another time, when he had planned to raise it externally. Now, he thought, I will enter you; I will become a part of you and then I will rise. You will go up with me, and we shall die on the shore. But you will be saved.

He made out the jagged ruins of the Black Cathedral. Broken into bits, he thought. Destroyed where I left you; rotten and unusable debris which serves no purpose and which no longer can block me, weak as I am. Because of all of you, he thought, I can function again. Can you hear me? He spoke distinctly. "Say if you can hear me."

"Yes we can."

"Yes."

"Yes." The answering voices rattled on and on; he counted them and they were all there, all alive and functioning as subforms of himself. "All right," he said, and triumph filled him as he dove directly at Heldscalla.

"Will we survive this?" Joe Fernwright asked. He felt fear.

You will, Glimmung thought. But not me. Raising his perimeters he extended himself so that his front end served as wide an area as possible. Now you are me, he thought, and I am you, Heldscalla. It has happened, despite The Book.

He held within him the sunken cathedral.

Now, he thought. He listened; he had ceased moving. Mr. Baldwin, he thought, and Miss Yojez, Mr. Dáq, Miss Fleg, Miss Reiss—can you hear me?

"Yes." Begrudging but genuine responses; he felt their presence, their agitation, as they held out against his pull. Come together, he told them. To survive we must go up, and to go up requires you to *act*. There is no other way. There never was.

"How can we act?" the voices asked.

Combine with me, Glimmung said. Add your skills, your capacities, your strengths . . . add everything to my mind. Mr. Baldwin; you move matter at a distance. Help me. Help them. Miss Yojez; you understand the art of removing objects from coral encrustation. Do that, now; unbind the coral reaches. Mr. Fernwright; you must knit the ceramic surfaces of the cathedral together . . . they are clay and you are the potter. Mr. Dáq; you are a hydraulic engineer. No, Dáq replied; I am a graphic archaeologist; I deal in recovered art objects. I can identify them, catalog them, and estimate their cultural value. Yes, Glimmung thought; it is Mr. Lunç who is the hydraulic engineer. I forgot. The similarity of names.

We will make our first run now! Glimmung told them, told the parts of himself who possessed separate identities. Probably we will sink back down. But we will try again. As long as we live? Mali Yojez asked. Yes, he thought. We will try as long as we are alive. Until the last of us is dead. But that's not fair, Harper Baldwin thought. Glimmung thought, You offered me everything you had; you yearned to help me when I lay dying. Now you are doing it. Be glad; rejoice. He grasped the uncut floor of the cathedral with his many somatic extensions. Before, he thought, when the Black Glimmung and the Black Cathedral were down here, I could not take the risk of lifting with my own girth. Now I can.

The lift failed. The cathedral remained rooted to the coral. Held fast by its mass, its weight, and bonds. He gasped, spent by the faulty effort. Everywhere within himself he ached, and all the separate voices cried out in panic and despair. And pain.

It doesn't wish to come, Joe Fernwright thought.

Is that so? Glimmung asked. How did you know that?

I found it out, Joe thought. When I came down here. I read it on the pot; remember?

Yes, Glimmung thought. I remember. He felt weary terror, the overwhelming submission which involved everything which came down here. Even himself. Once again, he thought. And then he thought, Faust always fails. But, he thought, I'm not Faust. You are, a multitude of voices came, a desperate din of defeat and refusal.

Let us go upward, Glimmung said. We are going. He felt the base of the cathedral resist. Perhaps you are right, he thought. I know I am, the voice came. It has happened before; it will happen again; it will always happen. But I can raise Heldscalla, Glimmung said to himself and to them. We can, all of us.

Using them, making them his arms, he lifted; he tugged the body of the cathedral to him and forced it to rise, against its own desires. Feeling it resist he felt bitterness and dismay. *I did not know this,* he thought. Perhaps this knowledge will kill me; perhaps this is what The Book meant. Perhaps, he thought, I should leave it down here; perhaps it is better the way it is.

It won't lift.

He tried again. No. It will not lift; I say it will not. At any time. For anyone. Under any combination of circumstances.

It will rise, Joe Fernwright said, when you are recovered from your injury, the damage done to you by the Black Cathedral.

"What?" he said, listening. Other voices joined Joe's. *When you are stronger. Wait until then.*

I must make myself stronger, he realized. Time must pass, authentic time over which I have no control. How can they know this when I do not? He listened, but heard no voices; they had quieted into silence as soon as he ceased striving. So be it, he decided. I will rise to the surface alone, and some day, not long from now, *I will try again.*

And once again, he decided, I will absorb you. All of you. Once more you will be parts of me as you are now. All right, the voices squeaked. But let us go; prove to us you can release us. I shall, he told them. And let himself rise to the surface.

Cold night air plucked at him and he saw feeble, distant stars.

On a wild shoreline, with nocturnal water birds striding about, he deposited the strident voices, he disgorged all of them, those whom he had incorporated, and then he lunged out again into the water—an aquatic world which was now safe: he could stay here forever and not be endangered by any hostile force. Thank you, Joe Fernwright, he thought, but now no answer came; internally he was again alone. So he spoke the words aloud, and, as he spoke, felt lonely. For a time he had been inhabited. But . . . it would come again, the warm, interior babble.

He examined his wounds, made himself comfortable in a half-submerged position, and waited.

Shivering, his feet in sandy mud, Joe Fernwright listened and heard Glimmung's voice. "Thank you, Joe Fernwright." He continued to listen, but there was no more.

He could see Glimmung, as the big creature lay a few hundred yards from shore. He would have killed us, Joe thought. And himself, too. In trying to bring up the cathedral. Thank god he listened.

"That was too close," Joe said to the other creatures near him, deployed here and there along the sandy beach. And especially to Mali Yojez, who huddled close to him, trying to get warm. "Much too close," he said, half to himself. He shut his eyes. Anyhow he let us go, he reflected. And now it's just a question of walking until we come to a house or a road. Unless he tries to get us back.

But that did not seem likely. Not, anyhow, for some time.

"Are you going to stay on Plowman's Planet?" Mali asked him. "You know what it means; he'll reabsorb all of us who stay here."

Joe said, "I'm staying."

"Why?"

"I want to see The Book proved wrong."

"It's already been proved wrong."

"I mean finally," Joe said. "Once and for all." As of now, he thought, it could still be right . . . because we don't know what will happen tomorrow or the day after. I could still kill Glimmung, he realized. In some indirect way.

But he knew that would not happen. It was too late. Like many things, it could not now be recalled. The Kalends were doomed. Their power was gone.

"But The Book was almost right," he said. Obviously the Kalends played the percentages. Generally, in the long run, they were correct. But in given instances—such as this—they were wrong. And this was important; this had to do with Glimmung's literal, physical death and the literal, physical raising of Heldscalla.

In relation to this, final events, such as the planet falling back into the sun from which it had arisen, did not really matter. They were too remote. In the final analysis the Kalends might be correct; their prophecies had to do with cosmic trends such as the laws of thermodynamics and terminal entropy. And, of course, Glimmung would eventually die. So would he himself. So would they all. But in the here and now Heldscalla waited for Glimmung to recover. And he would. And—the cathedral would come up from the water, as Glimmung planned.

"We were a polyencephalic entity," Mali said.

"Pardon?" Joe said.

"A group mind. Except that we were subordinate to Glimmung. But for a little while—" She gestured. "All of us, from at least ten star systems; we functioned as a single organism. In some ways it was exciting. To not be—"

"Alone," Joe said.

"Yes; it makes me realize how isolated each of us normally is, how cut off. Separated from everyone else . . . in particular separated from other life. That ended when Glimmung absorbed us. And we were no longer individual failures."

"It ended," Joe said, "but it's begun again. As of now."

Mali said, "If you stay here on Plowman's Planet, so will I."

"Why?"

"I like the group mind, the group will. As they say on your planet, this is where the action is."

"They haven't said that on Terra," Joe said, "for close to a hundred years."

"Our textbooks were very old," Mali said contritely.

Loudly, to the group members as they stood here and there, Joe said, "Okay; let's get started back to the Olympia Hotel. So we can get a hot bath and some dinner."

"And then sleep," Mali said.

He put his arm around her. "Or whatever else," he said, "that humanoids normally do."

16

Eight twenty-six-hour days later Glimmung asked the group to assemble under the hermetically sealed domes of the heated, illuminated staging center. The robot Willis checked the list as each arrived; when they had all come he notified Glimmung, and, collectively, they waited.

Of them all, Joe Fernwright had been the first to arrive. He made himself comfortable in one of the sturdy chairs and lit a cigarette made from Plowman's Planet grass. It had been a good week; he had seen a lot of Mali, and he had become friends with Nurb K'ohl Dáq, the warmhearted bivalve.

"Here's one they're telling on Deneb four," the bivalve said. "A freb whom we'll call A is trying to sell a glank for fifty thousand burfles."

"What's a freb?" Joe asked.

"A kind of—" The bivalve undulated with effort. "A sort of idiot."

"What's a burfle?"

"A monetary unit, like a crumble or a ruble. Anyhow, someone says to the freb, 'Do you really expect to get fifty thousand burfles for your glank?' "

"What's a glank?" Joe asked.

Again the bivalve undulated; this time it turned bright pink with effort. "A pet, a valueless lower life-form. Anyhow, the freb says, 'I got my price.' 'You got your price?' the inter-rogator interrogates. 'Really?' 'Sure,' the freb says. 'I traded it for two twenty-five-thousand-burfle pidnids.' "

"What's a pidnid?"

The bivalve gave up; it slammed its shell shut and withdrew into privacy and silence.

We're tense, Joe said to himself. Even Nurb K'ohl Dáq. It's getting to us all.

He rose to his feet, then; Mali had entered the room. "Here," Joe said, getting a chair for her.

"Thank you," Mali murmured as she seated herself. She seemed pale, and, when she lit a cigarette, her hands shook. "You should have lighted that for me," she said to him half jokingly and half accusingly. "I guess I'm the last to arrive." She glanced around the chamber.

"You were dressing?" Joe asked.

"Yes." She nodded. "I wanted to look right for what we're going to be doing."

Joe said, "How does one dress for polyencephalic fusion?"

"This." She rose to show him her green suit. "I've been saving this. For a special occasion. This is a special occasion." She reseated herself, crossed her long, trim legs, and smoked vigorously; obviously she was deep in thought: she hardly seemed aware of him.

Glimmung entered the room.

His form was new to them; Joe studied the prim, bag-shaped entity and asked himself why Glimmung had imitated this particular form of life. To what star system is this indig-enous? he wondered.

"My dear friends," Glimmung boomed. The voice had not changed. "First, I want you to know that I am fully recovered physically, although psychologically a trauma remains, mak-ing my memory erratic. Second, I have had tests run on all of you, without your knowledge and at no inconvenience to you, and I have the data which tell me that you, too, are physiologically in top form. Mr. Fernwright, I want to thank you especially for halting my premature efforts to raise the cathedral."

Joe nodded.

After a pause the bag-shaped object reopened its slitlike mouth and continued. "You all seem very quiet."

Getting to his feet Joe confronted Glimmung. "What are our chances of living through this?"

"Good," Glimmung said.

"But not excellent," Joe said.

Glimmung said, "I will make a compact with you. If I feel my strength waning—if I feel I can't make it—I will return to the surface and disgorge you."

"And then what?" Mali asked.

"And then," Glimmung said, "I will go back down and try once more. I will try until I can do it." Three morose eyes snapped open in the center of the baglike shape. "Is that what you mean?"

"Yes," the reddish jelly supported by a metal frame said.

"You are really only concerned with that?" Glimmung asked them. "Your personal safety?"

Joe said, "That's right." He felt odd, saying it. By this he had voided the dedicated atmosphere which Glimmung had brought with him; instead of the joint effort the individual lives had become paramount. And yet he had to do it. It was the consensus of the group. And, in addition, it was his own feeling.

"Nothing will happen to you," Glimmung said.

"Assuming," Joe said, "that you can get us up to the surface in time. And on dry land."

Glimmung, with his three centrally located eyes, regarded him for a protracted interval. "I did it once," he said.

Examining his wristwatch, Joe said, "Let's get started."

"Are you timing the universe," Glimmung asked, "to see if it is late? Are you giving breadth and measure to the stars?"

"I'm timing you," Joe said truthfully. "We have polled one another and our decision is to give you two hours."

" 'Two hours'?" The three eyes gaped at him in disbelief. "To raise Heldscalla?"

"That's right," Harper Baldwin said.

For a time Glimmung reflected. "You know," he said at last, "I can force polyencephalic fusion on you, on all of you, at any time. And I can refuse to release you."

"It won't come to that," the multilegged gastropod piped up. "Because even in fusion we can refuse to help. And if we don't give you that help you won't be able to do it."

The baglike entity swelled with pompous rage; a Luciferous sight: the indignation of an forty-thousand-ton creature contained by this frail vessel. Then gradually, Glimmung ebbed; he slid by degrees into comparative calm.

"It is now four-thirty in the afternoon," Joe said to Glimmung. "You have until six-thirty to raise Heldscalla and get us back on dry land."

Extending a pseudopodium, the baglike creature brought a copy of the Book of the Kalends from its pouch; it opened the volume and studied the text carefully. Then, thoughtfully, it closed the book and put it away in its pouch once more.

"What does it say?" the sharp-faced middle-aged woman asked.

Glimmung said, "It says I can't do it."

"Two hours," Joe said. "Less than two, now."

"I will not need two hours," Glimmung said, drawing himself up in dignity. "If I haven't done it in one hour, I will give up and deposit you back here." Turning, he stalked from the chamber and out onto the newly repaired wharf.

"Where do you want us?" Joe asked him, following him out of the hermetically sealed, warm region, into the late-afternoon cold.

"At the water's edge," Glimmung said. He sounded angry but at the same time contemptuous; the group's conditions seemed to have enlarged his determination.

Joe said, "Good luck."

The others flew, crawled, or walked out onto the wharf, now; as Glimmung had requested, they lined up at the water's edge. Glimmung surveyed them one last time, then descended the wooden ladder into the water. At once he disappeared beneath the surface; only circles of water and bubbles marked the place where he had gone. Possibly forever, Joe thought. He—and we—may never come back up.

Standing close to Joe, Mali said, "I'm scared."

"It won't be long, now," the plump woman with tangled baby-doll hair said.

"What's your specialty?" Joe asked her.

"Slabbing rock."

After that they waited in silence.

Fusion came to him as a monumental shock. And, he discovered, it came to the others the same way; the frightened babble of their composite voices washed over him—their voices and then the overpowering presence of Glimmung, his thoughts, his desires. And, Joe realized, his fears. Beneath the anger and contempt there was a core of anxiety that had not been evident before fusion. Now they all knew it . . . and Glimmung was aware of their knowledge; his thoughts altered as he deftly sought to evade their scrutiny.

"Glimmung is scared," the matronly woman declared.

"Yes, very scared," the timid little fellow piped.

"More," the quasiarachnid said, "than we are."

"Than some of us are," the immense dragonfly answered.

"Where are we?" the red-faced heavyset man demanded. "I'm disoriented already." Panic filled his voice.

Joe said, "Mali?"

"Yes." She seemed very near him, close enough for him to touch. But he had no manual extremities; like a worm in a cadaver he found himself, as before, rigidly placed within the magnasoma that was Glimmung. Separate motion was impossible, for any of them. They existed as mentational entities only . . . a weird sensation that he found unpleasant.

And yet—once again deeply augmented. Multiplied by all the others and, more than anything else, by Glimmung. He was helpless and in addition he constituted a supranormal organism whose potentialities were beyond calculation. For Glimmung, too, there had been a radical enlargement; Joe listened carefully to Glimmung's cerebral activity and marveled at the new acuity of it . . . acuity and power.

They dropped into the depths of the ocean.

"Where are we?" Harper Baldwin said nervously. "I can't see properly; I'm too far in. Can you see, Fernwright?"

Through Glimmung's eyes Joe saw the shape of Heldscalla grow before them. Glimmung moved rapidly, wasting no time; evidently he took the two-hour limit seriously. Reaching out, Glimmung sought to embrace the cathedral; he discharged, in a split second, his entire fund of energy in an attempt to hug the cathedral in a grip which could not be broken.

Suddenly Glimmung halted. Something rose from Heldscalla and confronted him, a dim figure. Glimmung's mice-scurrying thoughts poured over Joe, drenching him. From the thoughts Joe understood why Glimmung had ceased to move; he knew what the dim figure was.

A Fog-Thing. From antiquity. Which still lived. And it stood between Glimmung and Heldscalla.

Physically, literally, the Fog-Thing blocked the way.

"Questobar," Glimmung said. "You are dead."

The Fog-Thing said, "And, like everything else on this planet which is dead I live here, now. In Mare Nostrum. Nothing on the planet completely dies." The Fog-Thing raised its arm, then pointed directly at Glimmung. "If you raise Heldscalla from out of the depths to dry land, you will bring back to life the worship of Amalita and, indirectly, Borel. Are you prepared for that?"

"Yes," Glimmung said.

"And with it ourselves? As we were before?"

Glimmung said, "Yes."

"You no longer will be the dominant species on the planet."

"Yes," Glimmung said. "I know." Through him rapid thoughts traveled, but they were thoughts of tension, not of fear.

"And you still intend to raise the cathedral? Knowing this?"

"It must be put on dry ground," Glimmung said. "Back again where it belongs. Not down here in a world of decay."

The Fog-Thing stepped aside. "I will not stop you," it said.

Joy filled Glimmung; he rushed forward to seize Heldscalla, and with him they all plunged, too. All of them reached with Glimmung. All of them grasped the cathedral together. And, as they did so, Glimmung began to change. He devolved, rushing backward into time, becoming once more what he had long since ceased to be. He became powerful, wild, and wise. And then, as he lifted the cathedral, he changed again.

Glimmung became an enormous female creature.

Now the devolution reached the cathedral; it changed, too. In Glimmung's arms it became an encased fetus, a small, sleeping child-creature wrapped tightly in the cocoon whose strands enveloped it. Without effort, Glimmung raised it to the surface; all of them cried out in delight as, in a glimmering instant, the cathedral broke through into the cold late-afternoon sun.

Why the change? Joe wondered.

Glimmung answered. Because, she thought back to Joe, at one time we were bisexual. This part of me has been suppressed throughout the years. Until I obtained it again I could not make the cathedral my child. As it has to be.

Under the weight of the child-creature the dry ground sagged and failed; Joe felt the ground sink away under the majestic weight. But Glimmung did not seem alarmed; gradually, she released the cathedral, unwilling to let it go, to let it once again be separate from her. I am it, she thought, and it is part of me.

A clap of thunder sounded and rain began to fall. Quietly, heavily, the rain soaked into everything; water gushed from the cathedral and wound a tortuous route back to Mare Nostrum. Now, by degrees, the cathedral regained its customary form. The child-creature gave way to concrete and rock and basalt, to flying buttresses and a soaring Gothic arch. Once again the red-stained glass, derived from gold, shone in the erratic light of a rain-clouded sunfall.

It is done, Glimmung thought. Now I can rest. The great fisherman of the night has received its victory. Everything has been set in order once again.

Let us go, Joe thought. That ever yet remains.

"Yes!" others of them dinned. "Release us!"

Glimmung hesitated; Joe felt her conflicting thoughts ebb back and forth. No, she thought. Because of you I have great authority; if I release you I will sink again, dwindle into smallness.

You must, Joe thought. That was our compact.

True, Glimmung thought. But you have so much to gain as portions of me. We can function for a thousand years, *and none of us will be alone.*

"A vote," Mali Yojez said.

Yes, Glimmung thought. A vote among you, to see who wishes to remain within me and who chooses to separate into an individual entity.

I'll stay, Nurb K'ohl Dáq thought.

So will I, the quasiarachnid thought.

The vote continued; Joe listened to them, some of them electing to remain, some of them electing to break free. I want to be released, he said, when his time came to vote. At this Glimmung shuddered with dismay. Joe Fernwright, Glimmung thought. You are the best of them; won't you remain?

No, Joe thought.

He walked a shadowy shore with dark shapes looming, a dense and permanent swamp somewhere in the wilds of Plowman's Planet. How long had he been here? He did not know. Sometime before, he had been within Glimmung, and now he trudged painfully, the sharp sand lancing his feet as he struggled on.

Am I alone? he wondered. Halting, he peered into the twilight, trying to make out another life-form in his proximity.

The multilegged gastropod wriggled toward him. "I left with you," the gastropod said.

"Anyone else?" Joe asked.

The gastropod said, "In the final vote only the two of us. All the others remained. I consider it incredible, but it is so—they remained."

"Including Mali Yojez?"

"Yes," the gastropod said.

So that was that. He felt the weight of centuries on him; the task of raising the cathedral and now the loss of Mali were too much. "Do you know where we are?" he asked the gastropod. "I can't walk much farther."

"Neither can I," the gastropod said. "But there is a light to the north; I have drawn a paralactic fix on it and we are peregrinating in that direction. In another hour we should reach it, if I have computed our velocity correctly."

"I can't see the light," Joe said.

"My vision is superior to yours. You will see it in another twenty minutes. It winks almost out; it is very fragile. Probably a spiddle colony, I would guess."

"Spiddles," Joe said. "Are we going to live the rest of our life with spiddles? Is that how we wind up after leaving all the others and Glimmung?"

The gastropod said, "From there we can go by hovercar to the Olympia Hotel, where our possessions can be found. And then we can return to our own planets. We did a good job; we did what we came here for. We should rejoice."

"Yes," Joe said somberly. "We should rejoice."

"It was a great feat," the gastropod insisted. "You can see that the legends which maintain that Faust must fail are not only false in relation to reality, but in addition—"

"Let's talk about it," Joe broke in, "when we get back to the Olympia Hotel." He trudged on. After a moment of hesitation the multilegged creature followed after him.

"Is it very bad on your planet?" the gastropod inquired. "On Earth, as you call it?"

" 'On Earth,' " Joe said. "As it is in heaven."

"It is bad, then."

"Yes," Joe said.

The gastropod said, "Why don't you come with me to my world? I can get you a task . . . you're a pot-healer, aren't you?"

"I am," Joe said.

"We have many ceramics on Betelgeuse two," the gastropod said. "Your services would be in great demand."

"Mali," he said, half to himself.

Perceptively, the gastropod said, "I understand. But she's not coming; she's staying within Glimmung. Because, like the others, she is afraid to return to failure."

"I think I'll go to her planet," Joe said. "From what she said about it—" He ceased speaking, continued to trudge. "Anyhow," he said presently, "it would be better than Earth." And, he thought, I'd still be among humanoids. Maybe, he thought, I'll meet someone like Mali there. There is at least a chance.

In silence, the two of them continued on. Toward the far-off spiddle colony which, with each exhausted, halting, meager step, grew nearer.

"You know what I think your problem is?" the gastropod

said. "I think you ought to create a new pot, rather than merely patching up old ones."

"But," Joe said, "my father was a pot-healer before me."

"Observe the success of Glimmung's aspirations. Emulate him, who in his Undertaking fought and destroyed the Book of the Kalends and thus the tyrannic rule of fate itself. Be creative. Work against fate. Try."

Joe said, " 'Try.' " He had never thought about it, a new pot of his own creation. Technically, he knew how; he understood exactly how a ceramic piece was made.

"In the workshop Glimmung provided you," the gastropod said. "You have all the equipment and materials. With your knowledge and ability it should be a good pot."

"Okay," Joe said harshly. "Okay I will. I'll try."

In the new, gleaming workshop he stood, the overhead lights flooding down on him. He studied the major workbench, the three sets of waldoes, the self-focusing magnifying glasses, the ten separate heat-needles, and—every glaze: every tint, shade, and hue. The weightless area; he inspected that. The kiln. Jars of wet clay. And the potter's wheel, electrically driven.

Hope welled up within him. He had all he needed. Wheel, clay, glazes, kiln.

Opening a jar he got out of it a dripping lump of gray clay; he carried the clay to the potter's wheel, started it turning, and plopped the clay down dead center. And on my first try, he said to himself, feeling pleased. Using his strong thumbs he began to dig into the lump, meanwhile, with his fingers, drawing the lump into something high. And virtually symmetric. Higher and higher the mound grew, and deeper and deeper his thumbs sank into it, hollowing out the center.

At last it was done.

He dried the clay in an infrared oven and then, taking a simple glaze, he ornamented the pot. One more color? He selected a second glaze, and that was enough. Time to go into the kiln.

He placed it in the already hot kiln, bolted the door, and seated himself at the workbench to wait. He had plenty of time. A lifetime, if necessary.

An hour later the kiln's timer pinged. The kiln had shut off; the pot was done.

With an asbestos glove, he tremblingly reached into the still-hot kiln and brought out the tall, now blue-and-white pot. His first pot. Taking it to a table, under direct light, he set it down and took a good look at it. He professionally appraised its artistic worth. He appraised what he had done, and, within it, what he would do, what later pots would be like, the future of them lying before him. And his justification, in a sense, for leaving Glimmung and all the others. Mali most of all. Mali whom he loved.

The pot was awful.